A PARCEL OF DIAMONDS

By the same author

From Oaks to Avocets

A

PARCEL

OF

DIAMONDS

JOHN WALLING

Riparian Publishing

Published by Riparian Publishing
5 Tonnant Way
Great Grimsby
North East Lincolnshire
Telephone 01472 879958

ISBN 0 9523848 1 7

British Library Cataloguing in Publication Data.
A catalogue record for this book is available from the British Library.

Printed and bound in the UK by Antony Rowe Ltd,
Bumper's Farm. Chippenham Wiltshire
Typesetting by Riparian Publishing, Great Grimsby,
North East Lincolnshire.
Cover by David Lawson, Graphic Designer, Unit 4, Cleethorpes Enterprise
Centre, Humberston, North East Lincolnshire.

To David

CONTENTS

ALL THAT GLITTERS....

CHAPTER ONE

But for the war, Detective Inspector Alistair McIntosh would have retired from the force. By 1939 he had served his required thirty years to enable him to live a comfortable life on a well earned pension, but was persuaded to remain in the Glasgow Central Division until, 'the end of hostilities,' as his superintendent had put it. If the war was going to go on for a long time, it was anticipated that a shortage of new recruits would develop, and, together with the inevitability of increased duties, it would put a great strain on the police resources. So, along with others who had served their time, he was asked to stay - although he knew that he couldn't really refuse as the request had come from very high authority.

At the beginning of 1945, the armies of the United Kingdom and the United States were closing in on the remains of the German Army, and all but the Third Reich were confident that the Allies would soon be victorious. By the middle of April, there was left little more than a central corridor in Germany unoccupied, including Berlin. Inspector McIntosh was looking forward to a quieter life, and had promised himself that he would retire as soon as the last shot had been fired. He scanned the newspapers eagerly, almost ticking off the days to his well-earned rest. He hoped that the only major case left to deal with could be given to the U.S. Army authorities in the country to solve: the bloated body of an American soldier had emerged from the depths of the Clyde close to the bridge at Bothwell where the river crossed under the A74, twelve miles from Glasgow south east of the city. It seemed of little consequence to Alistair, and he thought that it was probably the result of yet another case of trouble in the inevitable conflict between black and white Americans. However, he was given the task of looking into the circumstances of the death, knowing that if the soldier had been stabbed, there would be very little chance of finding out who had done it. He took his time driving the black police saloon to the hospital mortuary where the body had been taken.

"Have you discovered the cause of death?" the inspector asked.

"There's some doubt about it, Alistair," said the police pathologist. "It's difficult after all this time, but I've found some bruising either side of the neck which points to someone grabbing him there and squeezing hard."

"You mean he's been strangled."

"Well, could be, but the pressure on either side of his neck could have stopped the blood from flowing to his brain, which would kill him. But there's no doubt that he was dead before he was put into the water."

"How long has he been there?"

"Oh, I would think at least three months."

"Is that all you can tell me?" pleaded the inspector.

"Well, he's male, but then you knew that, about twenty-five years of age, an American G.I., but then you knew that also." He was grinning at the inspector.

"Okay, stop dragging it out. What have we got to go on?" Alistair was beginning to lose his patience. He wanted to go home and leave all this to the U.S.Army to deal with.

The pathologist looked at the inspector over the top of his spectacles. "Oh yes, I almost forgot," he teased, and held out his hand to the inspector. "Nothing in his pockets, but this identity tag

2

was still around his neck."

It was a week before Alistair received the information which he had asked for. The body was that of a Private Joseph Peabody, who had been reported as a deserter from the 1st American Army in about the middle of December. A lieutenant in the Administration Office in London had telephoned him to tell him the news, and said that they would appreciate any co-operation that could be given by the police in Glasgow in trying to solve who had killed him.

Detective Inspector Alistair McIntosh's heart sank. This is just what he could have done without during his last days in the force. He had visions of his retirement being delayed even further. He would try the newspapers first, and gave the story to both the local press, and the national papers, asking them to make a bit of a headline out of it, otherwise it would not be seen among the other more important stories about the last days of the war. He would ask the news editors to appeal to their readers for anyone who knew the American or who might have seen him. After all, many girls became very friendly with the American soldiers. Fortunately, the "Daily Mirror" somehow managed to obtained a photograph of the soldier from the American Army Headquarters and made a bit of a splash about the story in the centre pages.

Cornelius Hill, the landlord of the "Cricketer's Arms" in the village of Western, in Dorset, was an avid reader of the "Daily Mirror." After first finding out what Jane was up to in the popular cartoon strip, and to see whether she had removed her dress yet again, he turned to the middle pages and saw the headline, "American Soldier Strangled." The story told how an American G.I. called Joe Peabody, had been found in the Clyde about three months after being murdered, and that the police were calling for anyone who had known him or had seen anything suspicious in the area about that time.

"Hey, Liz," he called to his attractive barmaid, "isn't this that Joe who used to come here, that American you....er...knew?" He was aware that she more than just knew him, but quickly decided to say no more so as not to embarrass her. "You never did tell me what happened after you went to Scotland with him. I think you'd better tell the police what you know, don't you?" he suggested, handing her the paper for her to read.

Elizabeth Harrison looked hard at the photograph. It wasn't a very good likeness of Joe, but the name and description of the man she had known fitted exactly. She had indeed travelled with him in the Glasgow train, and he had got off at Carlisle station for what she had thought was going to be just a few minutes. She couldn't possibly tell her employer all that had happened after that.

"He left me on the train when he got out at Carlisle, and I never saw him again," she explained. "The reason I stayed in Glasgow is that I met a boy in the Fleet Air Arm, and we had a good time together for a few days, and that's all."

The landlord had only enquired on one occasion as to why Joe had not come back with her from her trip to Scotland, but she had told him at the time that she wasn't going to see him again, and he knew enough about his pretty barmaid not to have asked her any further questions. He now believed that she had just told him the truth, but wondered what he ought to do. "What an end for poor old Joe", he said sadly, "I suppose I'd better let the police know that he used to come here."

Liz began to panic. "Why do that? What can you tell them? He had no friends, only me, and how would that look to the police. In the paper, it said that he'd been strangled before he was dumped into the river. I wasn't involved with his death, and I didn't know who was, but do you think that the police would believe that I had nothing to do with it if they found out that I'd been to Scotland with him? You didn't tell anyone else where I had gone at the

4

time, did you?"

The landlord shook his head. "You asked me not to and I kept my word. I told everyone that you'd been to Scotland like you said, to see your aunt."

"So you won't say anything about either of us to the police will you?. It won't help them."

Cornelius noticed that she was giving him one of her beseeching looks, pleading for him to do what she had asked. "Well, let's hope that none of my customers recognise him from the story in the paper. If they do, I'll have to tell them that we've already reported it," he said, somewhat reluctantly.

She gave her employer a kiss on his cheek, which ended the matter as far as he was concerned, and he turned back to the front page of his newspaper to read about how the Allies were closing in on Berlin, and how the war in Europe would soon be over.

Liz went to her room to go over everything that happened since she had last seen Joe. She recalled that before she had returned to Dorset after her stay in Glasgow, she had been questioned by the police at Carlisle, and they would now, no doubt, tell the officer in charge of the investigation in Glasgow that she had perhaps known more about this American soldier than she had told them at the time. She then thought about Howard, the sailor whom she had met on the train and the close relationship they had formed with one another. He had not been out of her mind since she returned to London. He had been so kind and helped her in every way. She had wanted so much to see him again. Now she began to worry what he might tell the police if they went to interview him at the Royal Navy Air Station at Paisley where he had been stationed, and probably was still. In view of all the events that had taken place, she began to feel very frightened and lay down on the bed, her body shaking. The last time she had felt as scared as this was four years ago in London. She recalled that time and everything that had happened afterwards.

CHAPTER TWO

Elizabeth Harrison was born in a terraced house in Earl Street close to Liverpool Street Station. Her parents had been killed in the first daylight raid on London during the second year of the war. She had been working as an trainee ladies hairdresser in a shop in the City at the time when the air raid siren had sounded, and had spent the next few hours, along with hundreds of others, in the Leicester Square Underground station sheltering from the bombing. She would never forget that day, and the feeling of horror when she finally managed to reach home to find the houses in Earl Street reduced to rubble. There was no sign of the house where she had been born and was met by the street warden to tell her that both her parents were dead.

She had been only in her sixteenth year and had matured very quickly after that. After the funeral, she left London, and went to live with an aunt in a village in Dorset where she had managed to get a job as a barmaid in a local public house.

She was a pretty girl with a good figure. Her long straight auburn hair which almost reached her shoulders, ended in a neatly groomed roll at the bottom. She had an infectious smile and soon the customers loved her. The trouble was that one or two of the soldiers took advantage of her and she became involved with them. The landlord turned a blind eye to her 'goings on', as he called it, and, as long as it did not interfere with her work, he didn't complain. After all, having an attractive barmaid did bring business into his pub, and if he'd been a younger man, he wouldn't have minded getting involved with her himself. However, local gossip soon put an end to the good relationship that she and her aunt had enjoyed, and Liz was told to leave the house. Fortunately, the landlord of the pub where she worked had a small cottage which he said she could rent while she remained in his employ.

Life in the village went on happily, with the British soldiers filling the pub at weekends. Two or three years later, the American soldiers, who had arrived in England, also began visiting the village local public houses on a regular basis. Liz became very friendly with a tall handsome G.I. called Joe. He brought her things that young girls at that time found it almost impossible to obtain, showering her with gifts of nylons, perfume, and chocolates, and making her feel very special. For the first time since her parents had died she had met someone who appeared to respect her, and her relationship with Joe made her realise that she was wasting her life. He repeatedly told her that he loved her, and she was enchanted by him. She had never previously experienced the wonderful exciting feelings she had when they made love, and wanted to be with him all the time. He, however, only managed to see her at intervals, each one seeming an eternity to Liz.

When they were together they often talked about themselves, Liz opening her heart to him about the life she had been living since her parents had been killed. Joe was very understanding about what she had been through, and made light of what had been her unfortunate way of life before they had met.

He told her about his Ranch in Texas and how he would take her to his home in America when the war was over. "You'll love it there, honey, and we'll get married and have lots of kids" - and she, in her naivety, believing every word he told her. But soon, a feeling of mistrust began to sour their relationship.

He admitted to her how he had acquired the things he had

brought, most of which were stolen. She couldn't bring herself to condone the things that he had done until, finally, she begged him not to bring any more gifts unless he got them honestly.

During 1944, his visits to the pub stopped, and rumours spread that the invasion of France was imminent. From the beginning of May, Liz never saw or heard from him again until he suddenly appeared at her cottage door about eight months later, towards the end of December.

"I'm back, honey," he shouted, raising his arms above his head, then closing them tightly around her waist. He was holding a bottle of Bollinger in his hand which she felt pressing against her back.

"Just wait 'till I get the dern cork out of this," he said, now holding the bottle in front of her, "then we'll celebrate in style."

Liz knew exactly what he meant, as he had often used that phrase when he wanted to make love. After three good glasses of champagne she didn't care. However, it wasn't quite the same as it had been when they had first met. Even while they were making love she couldn't stop herself from wondering why he was here, and how he had acquired that rare bottle of champagne.

Sometime later as they lay on the bed, she pointed to the now empty bottle and asked, "Where did you get it, Joe?"

"Does it matter honey? Stop worryin'. Anyway, I've gotten something for yer far more interestin' than that bottle of bubbly." He stubbed out his cigarette in the ash tray by the side of the bed.

She lay there looking at him and fear came over her. She was certain that whatever he was going to show her was going to be the result of something either dishonest or unpleasant he had done. She still had presents unopened that he had brought her previously, her conscience not allowing her to enjoy them knowing them to have been stolen. When he began telling her not to worry, it usually meant that she would probably need to, so she had a good idea of what he was about to tell her. "Whatever it is that you have, Joe," Liz said quietly, looking into his eyes, "I need to know how you got it, and, while you're at it, you can tell me where the champagne came from as well."

Joe knew that he wouldn't be able to deceive her, but wondered how she would react when he told her that he was not only a deserter, but also was wanted for murdering a Belgian he had robbed of some diamonds.

Liz listened as he unravelled the mystery, her face losing its colour and almost too scared to speak when he had finished his story. He got off the bed and feeling inside his tunic, produced the bag of diamonds he had stolen. Without saying another word he tipped the shiny stones on to her bare skin. One settled snugly into her navel.

"My, that looks pretty," he quipped. "You oughta leave it there for ever," and he gave a hearty chuckle, then kissed her. "If you're a good girl, half of those are yours," he added.

Liz opened her eyes wide, forgetting for a second how he had come by them, and hardly daring to breathe for fear of spilling all the diamonds off her body and on to the bed. She then asked excitedly, "How much are they worth, Joe?" It was if she was trying to evaluate them against the life that had been taken.

"Are you ready for this, Liz? At least you won't faint lyin' down."

He paused, mainly for dramatic effect, then bent down to whisper in her ear, drawing out his words very slowly, "Probably well over two-hundred-thousand dollars. That's about twenty-five thousand in your English pounds.....and that's each, honey."

Liz stared at him incredulously, swallowing hard. "You must be joking!" she exclaimed.

"How about that?" Joe said grinning. "They're worth a dern lot more but we'll probably only git less than half their real value. I'm waitin' for a phone call from Glasgow confirmin' the real figure."

He thought it best not to tell Liz anything about the

arrangements he had made with the Scotsman he befriended in the hospital ship on the way over from France.

Liz got up off the bed and dressed hurriedly without saying a word. Joe had killed for the stones and was also wanted by the Army for desertion. If he got caught it would be no more than he deserved. But £25,000! It was an awful lot of money she thought, and it would be all for her. She had never had a real break in her life, and that amount of money would make her rich. If she went along with him, she would never have any more worries, and no one would ever be able to trace where the money had come from. It was an opportunity that came once in a lifetime and, by the time she was dressed, she had decided to go along with whatever arrangements Joe had made.

"When will you find out, and how will you get the money?" she asked.

Joe explained that the person he was dealing with would be telephoning the pub in a few weeks time. "I'll still be here until that happens, then we'll go to Glasgow to git the cash for the diamonds. That'll be early in the new year, so you'll just have to be patient 'till then, honey."

She guessed that Joe had almost certainly planned to lie low afterwards until the war was over, then go back to the States, but she now had no desire to go with him. She decided that she would continue with their relationship, then probably go back to London and start a new life there after she had received her share of the money. She thought it best to keep all this to herself until all the arrangements had been completed.

The next couple of weeks behind the bar of the pub were very busy ones with all the celebrations of Christmas and the New Year. All the customers were more relaxed than in previous years, anticipating joyfully that the war in Europe was almost at an end. Even Joe wasn't questioned by any of the customers as to why he was there, and was treated as something of a hero by the local population.

In the second week in January, Joe received his awaited telephone call from the Scottish soldier, Andy McKern, who had been arranging everything for him as Joe had instructed him to do. Andy told him about the hotel he had booked in St. Enoch's Square, the address of the man he was to do business with in Glasgow, and how he had made an appointment for eight o'clock on the following Wednesday evening for them to meet. Andy also confirmed that, subject to a final satisfactory examination, the amount he had estimated for the diamonds he had examined on the boat coming over, had proved to be about right. He didn't tell Joe that he'd made his own agreement with his contact, Charlie MacKenzie, to receive £10,000 for himself.

Joe knew now that he was being offered far less than they were worth, otherwise the amount would not have been agreed so easily, but he was more than satisfied with the figure, and was anxious to get rid of the diamonds as quickly as possible. He explained to Andy, that Liz would be coming with him as arranged, and that they would be travelling on the six-o'clock train to Glasgow on Friday evening, arriving there early next morning, and that they would be going straight to the hotel. He still thought it best not to tell Liz about Andy, as he reckoned she probably didn't really want to know any more than she knew already, but he did tell her about all the arrangements that had been made should anything go wrong.

Going to London was a risk that Joe was taking, and he knew it. He had no other clothes apart from his uniform, but fortunately there were a number of other American soldiers in the City when they arrived on Friday afternoon to catch the train from Euston Station. He had put the diamonds in a small attache case and had given it to Liz, telling her to board the train before him and he would follow later. In that way, he explained, they wouldn't be seen together, and, if he was unfortunately arrested by the

Military Police - who appeared to be everywhere - the diamonds would not be discovered. What Joe had not told her, was that he had arranged to meet Andy briefly at Carlisle to confirm that everything was still as arranged, but would tell her after he had seen him.

Liz boarded the train, found an empty carriage and pulled down the blinds. She put her feet against the door to prevent anyone else from entering, and waited for Joe with breathless excitement.

Joe waited until the train was about to leave, then ran along the platform and boarded the train at the very last minute.

CHAPTER THREE

Marine Commando Andy McKern had been specially trained to serve with the 1st Special Service Brigade, and under the command of Lord Lovat, had landed with his comrades on Sword Beach on D.Day. During the following six months, as the Allies advanced through France and Belgium, the fighting had been intense. His unit was usually in the forefront of most of the attacks, and he had considered himself to have been extremely fortunate not to have been even wounded from either shrapnel or bullet during this time. However, during a brief reconnoitre with two other marines in order to try and ascertain the enemy's position at a particularly troublesome spot, he had been hit by a German sniper's bullet, and was now aboard a hospital ship returning to England.

The bullet had shattered the bone in his left shoulder damaging the nerves right down the arm to the end of his fingers. The limb was practically useless, and he had been told to keep it close to his body in a large sling until he could get it seen to by a surgeon. He had been instructed to report to a Glasgow hospital for extensive operations to be carried out to try and repair the damage that had been done. Andy knew that his war was almost certainly over, and he was looking forward to be able to get back to Scotland as soon as possible to enable him to return to his old job in the city.

Andy had been an assistant to a reputable jeweller who had a shop in the centre of Glasgow but, always ready to make a little on the side, he was friendly with a so-called diamond merchant who rented small premises in a back-alley off Sauchiehall Street. Charlie MacKenzie's small shop was well known. It was the place where young couples of limited means could purchase diamond engagement rings for a very low price - at least, they looked like real diamonds but were really just costume jewellery. However, Charlie MacKenzie didn't deceive any of his customers. He always told them exactly what they were purchasing, but if there was a shady deal to be done in diamonds in Glasgow, both Andy and Charlie MacKenzie were almost certain to be involved.

Why Andy had volunteered to join a specialist section of commandos was something he had often wondered about. Although he was only five feet and a few inches tall, he was a stocky little man with a fine pair of strong legs of which he was proud. He'd often told the story that his lack of height gave him an advantage in the fighting, as he considered that most of the bullets fired in his direction would go over his head. However, until this last one found its target, the risks he had taken had been exciting and challenging, and he had experienced feelings not unlike those he had had when he had been involved in those illicit deals with Charlie MacKenzie before the war, but the danger then was of being arrested, not shot at!

Many of the friends he had made while serving in the army had been killed, and he considered himself to have been very lucky not to been wounded before this last encounter. Although he had felt anger at the time and used some very strong language about the German who had shot him, he was pleased that he was still alive and finished with the fighting.

After leaving the harbour at Dieppe, the hospital ship he was on was only a couple of miles out to sea before he was leaning over the rails, and wondering why he'd bothered to have such a big breakfast. He had never been a good sailor, and when they had all gone over the English Channel on D.Day, he had been sea-sick for a good part of the way during that long and horrendous sea voyage. On that day, with heavy seas and a strong wind, many of the men had also suffered in the same way, although then it hadn't only been the pitch and toss of the boat which had caused the nausea, but the fear of what lay ahead on those fortified beaches, and whether they would still be alive at the end of that first, and what proved to be, terribly long, day.

Due to the Allies' supremacy both in the air and on the sea as they crossed the English Channel on this particular journey, there was no need for that sort of anxiety for their safety, and it was now only the movement of the ship which caused him to feel ill. He pulled his coat around him with his one good arm, trying to keep himself warm in the icy cold December air, and, as he did so, he was aware of another unfortunate victim only a few yards along the rail suffering in the same way as himself. He recognised the olive-coloured, and well-tailored uniform of an American GI. The American soldier moved along the rail towards him and put his hand on Andy's good shoulder.

"How yer doin' fella? I'm Joe," he said in a tired and weak voice. His face looked drawn and bloodless. He too was shivering.

Andy mumbled his own name and, noticing the American's pale complexion, remarked, "Och! You look as bad as I feel."

They stood for a while watching the white crests of the black waves dancing in the moonlight, until the American said that he was feeling a little better and suggested that they ought to go back inside the ship and into the warmth.

"I think I'd rather die of sea-sickness inside the ship than dern well freeze to death out here. What d'yer say, Andy?"

The Scotsman agreed. "Aye, I suppose it's worth risking."

Once inside, they sat quietly for a while to get the circulation working back into their cold bodies before agreeing that if they talked to each other it may take their minds off the ship's movement.

"Did yer come over on D.Day, an' what'yer done to yourself,

Andy?" Joe pointed to the Scotsman's sling and heavily bandaged shoulder, "or was it one son-of-a-bitch German gave it to yer?" he asked.

Andy had no intention of giving this fellow his life history, but explained briefly his time spent in the army as modestly as possible. He was not particularly fond of Americans anyway and was careful not to give away any secrets in case the fellow turned out to be different from what he appeared. However, he could see no harm in telling him about his civilian life in Glasgow, and when he was in the jewellery trade before he went into the army. As he talked it reminded him how much that he wanted to get back and forget all about the war, and it also took his mind off the fact that he was on board a ship with thousands of feet of water below the plimsoll line. He was also aware of the reputation of some G.Is to 'shoot-a-line', so he thought that there would be no harm in boasting that he knew enough about diamonds to be almost an expert. "I'll be able t'get a job quite easy in the trade when I get oot o' the army, so, Joe, if you want any cheap diamonds, I'm your man," Andy joked.

Joe listened intently to what his newly-found acquaintance was saying, especially when he talked about his knowledge of diamonds. It was a lucky coincidence that he had met someone who knew something about them, and Joe had a bag full of them inside his coat pocket. Could he trust him? Would he know their value if he showed them to him? But would he want to know how he had acquired them? Andy had joked about how he had got involved with some shady deals in the jewellery trade, even boasted about it. Surely he could trust him if he offered him a good deal. Joe had wondered previously how he could get rid of the diamonds, and now luck had brought this devious character to him who could probably help him to sell them.

"Could yer put a value on some diamonds by just looking at 'em?" Joe asked.

"Well, nae really," Andy explained. "Diamonds are a very complicated business, and valuing 'em depends on many factors."

"Couldn't yer even gi'me a very rough estimate of say a handful?" the American asked.

"I could tell if they were genuine or no', but the value wi' depend if they were cut correctly, the colour, and a number of other things which determines the price. Why d'you want to know?" Andy had heard of some soldiers collecting souvenirs as they went into the towns who were dealt with very severely if they were caught, but that didn't stop some of the more unscrupulous soldiers from stealing. However, if this fellow had a few diamonds, he would be interested, and maybe could do well for himself at the same time.

"Somebody gave me some and then gotten themselves killed," Joe explained. It was partly true, but he wasn't going tell a stranger what had really happened. "If yer could sell 'em for me, well that'd be swell. How about it buddy?"

"Where are they? Can I see 'em?" Andy tried to sound very calm because he knew that if he had shown surprise, he would have lost Joe's confidence in being able to trust him. He had dealt with situations like this before. "I dinna have my wee eye-glass with me, but do you nae think that we can try to find somewhere wi' a better light?"

"I've got the packet inside my tunic. I've left my bag over there with the rest of my things," Joe said, pointing to a slightly better lit area, "so maybe we could er.. use that corner?"

Andy corrected him. "It's nae a packet, it's what we call in the trade, a parcel of diamonds, but there's nae enough light there to enable me to examine them carefully."

Joe rummaged around in his bag and produced a large metal torch. It clinked against a bottle, and Joe just winked and whispered, "Two bottles o' champagne. Keep it quiet. Okay?"

Andy wondered what else he might be carrying: diamonds and

champagne were enough to cause him to suspect that this fellow was not telling him the truth about how he had acquired these things. If he asked, he expected that this American would tell him that someone gave him the champagne as well!

Joe looked around to ensure that no one else could see what they were doing before taking the bag out from the inside pocket of his tunic. He spread the diamonds out over his handkerchief and Andy couldn't believe his eyes. There were far more than he had expected to see, estimating that there must have been two-hundred or more stones: all of different sizes, but some even quite large. He knew immediately that these hadn't been given to this American, but thought it best to say nothing at this stage.

"I'd need a magnifying glass to examine them properly," Andy explained under his breath. "I'm nae an expert, but there must be thousands and thousands of pounds worth here." Without taking his eyes off the diamonds under the torchlight, he added, "If we could weigh 'em to determine the amount of carats, then I could perhaps gie a price nearer to their value." Andy was aware that he would be nowhere near the real value as each one would have to be examined carefully to ascertain their true worth, but he quickly saw that he could be on to good thing here, as the Yank obviously knew absolutely nothing about the value of the stones he had.

"Where did your friend get 'em?" Andy asked innocently. He would be intrigued to hear Joe's answer but at the same time was determined to handle the situation carefully.

Joe had anticipated the question and was ready with his answer. A minimum of truth would be all that was necessary. "Antwerp, I think he'd said."

Andy was now more convinced than ever that he wasn't being told the truth, but the place of origin seemed correct. "Och, then that explains it. A puckle of the larger ones are uncut. Antwerp is the centre of uncut diamonds."

Joe was perplexed. "What's a puckle?"

Andy had used the Scottish word to confuse him. "It's a few to you Joe."

Joe was astonished at Andy's first estimate of their worth - thousands and thousands of pounds he had said. He decided to act quickly. "If yer can git a good price for 'em, ten per cent's yours."

Andy nodded his head, partly in agreement of the ten per cent, and partly because he was confident that he could find a buyer. "They should hae some accurate scales in the dispensary on board for weighing ounces, although, they won't be troy weight scales. Let's go and see."

They found what they were looking for, and Andy was not surprised to discover that the weight was almost eight ounces including the bag. He said nothing until they went back to the quiet corner they had left, then he began to try to calculate the figure which he thought would satisfy the American. Even by just looking at them, he knew that being genuine they would be worth a great deal of money.

"Jewels are usually measured in troy weight", Andy began excitedly making his calculations with his eyes tightly closed. "And if I remember correctly, there are twenty-four carats to the troy ounce, twelve ounces to the pound as opposed to sixteen avoirdupois, which means that allowing for the bag to weigh aboot an ounce, it leaves something in the region of seven ounces of diamonds to be converted to troy weight... multiplied by say an average price per carat.." - he did the calculations in his head so as not to reveal the figure he had in mind, and then deliberately divided the answer by four so that Joe would only be told a figure of about a quarter of what he had worked out - "so, you might get," he looked at Joe for his reaction, "aboot £50,000."

Joe gave a long drawn out whistle of disbelief. It was obvious that he had had no idea how Andy had done the calculations, but he had been impressed, and was satisfied as to the figure he had given. "Are you sure that you'll be able to git that amount of dough for 'em?"

Charlie MacKenzie sprang to Andy's mind immediately. "I think I ken a jeweller in Glasgow who'd be interested."

Joe's mind was working fast as he replaced the stones into the bag and put them back into his tunic pocket. After a few minutes he had it all figured out. "Here's what I wanna yer to do," he said. "I ain't gonna give yer the diamonds, but get that price confirmed from yer contact in Glasgow after tellin' him what you've seen. Then, second, while you're up there, book me a room at a small hotel for two using the name of Harrison. That's my girl-friend's name, and I'll be takin' her with me pretendin' to be on honeymoon. That'll take any suspicion off why we're there, so don't give the hotel any warnin' who'll be comin' except that we're a married couple, okay? Here, take one of these bottles with you to give to the hotel for us to celebrate with when we arrive. I don't expect the hotel will have any to spare - that is if they have any at all!" He handed one of the champagne bottles to Andy. "We'll follow later on, an' then don't waste any time in sein' that jeweller friend of yours. He'll be making a good profit I suspect, so yer can take yer cut from him - I guess they're worth a lot more than yer said, so I'll expect nothin' less than the figure you've given me, okay? Oh, and by the way, make sure yer tell him I'll want cash."

Andy didn't need to think very long about what Joe had said. He was certain that the value of the stones would be at least £200,000, and, when the uncut stones were evaluated correctly, probably a lot more, but he would keep all that to himself. Before he could agree, Joe added, "There's only one condition, an' that is, yer don't ask any questions."

Andy shuddered a little at the thought of what Joe might do if he found out that he had given him such a low figure of their real value, but at the same time, the whole arrangements sounded very suspicious. Why all the secrecy? He didn't particularly like Americans, and he certainly didn't trust this one. He wondered whether he might have deserted his unit after stealing the diamonds himself. No one in his right mind would have given them to him like he had said, and it sounded too much of a coincidence for the person who had given them to him to be killed soon afterwards. However, because of their true value, he wasn't going to argue with any conditions that Joe put on the deal, but he would like to try and find out a bit more about his acquaintance.

"There is one question I'd like t'ask before I agree," Andy said, "and it's nothing to dae wi' the diamonds."

"Fire away," Joe said confidently.

"What are you da'en on this hospital ship? Why are you going to England? and why hiv you left your unit? You don't appear to be wounded!"

The questions took Joe by surprise. "I thought yer said you were dern well goin' to ask only one question. I just counted three!"

"A'right then," Andy interjected, "I want to ken what risks I am taking if I agree to help you."

Joe contemplated whether he ought to tell him the truth. The Scotsman had said, *if* he agreed to help him. Joe could not afford to let this opportunity go by, and it was doubtful whether he would get a better chance of getting rid of the diamonds than this. He hesitated for a while before he said anything, wondering whether he ought to tell a complete stranger the whole story of how he managed to obtain them, but it could be the way to ensure that the Scotsman would help him - so he decided to tell him everything. "Okay, Jock, I'll level with yer, if that's the only way yer going to help me."

Andy hated being called Jock, especially by a Yank!

"The diamonds are mine," Joe continued, "an' I stole 'em from a jeweller in Antwerp." He waited to see if there was any reaction from the Scotsman.

There was none. Andy didn't flinch. He'd dealt with people who brought him stolen goods when he had worked in Glasgow before the war, but he wasn't prepared for what came next from this unscrupulous American.

"This crafty Belgian had kept 'em hidden from the Germans throughout the occupation, an' when I called in to his premises for a small souvenir, it was by chance that he'd just recovered 'em from where he'd had 'em hidden. I couldn't believe my luck as he told me how he'd deceived the Bosch, but he refused to give me even one small diamond, so the only way I could get 'em was to bump him off. I don't believe anybody saw me, and I hoped that when his body was recovered the people would think that he was killed an' robbed by the Jerries before they left. So, my Scottish friend, no one knows about 'em except you, an' no one knows I'm here, right? Does that satisfy yer?" He looked hard at the Scotsman and saw hardly any reaction to his confession. "So what yer gonna do?"

Andy's heartbeat considerably increased in pace as Joe's last remark sounded more like a threat than a question. He tried to ignore it. "So you're wanted for desertion, theft and possibly murder?" he said bluntly. "Phew! the people I do business with!" and gave the American a weak smile. He could see that he was dealing with someone who would stop at nothing to get what he wanted. This American had committed one murder, and no doubt would do another. Andy realised that he would have to be careful, but now that he knew the truth, he had little option but to do as Joe wanted. After all, he would make a lot of money in the deal, although once he had accepted his role as middleman and seller of the stones, he would then be an accomplice after the fact to Joe's crimes.

Joe was sure that his gamble of telling Andy everything had paid off, and that his plan would succeed. He felt quite safe and secure in having done so.

"After I've contacted my man in Glasgow, how do I get in touch with you to tell you everything is a'right?" Andy asked, "You hinna even given me your full name."

"And yer don't need to know it, my friend. Just Joe will do for now," and he began writing something down on a piece of paper which he handed to Andy. "Yer can get in touch with me by callin' this number, and ring me as soon as things are arranged. I dunna want yer to do anythin' until early in the new year as I wanna lie low for a while. Can you remember everythin' I've told yer?" He looked at Andy, and then partly under his breath told him in no uncertain terms, "An' I think you'll be wise to keep that telephone number and our conversation to yourself - Okay Jock?"

Andy understood immediately what he had meant by that. "Can I have anither wee look at those diamonds before you go," he asked.

Joe couldn't wait to get to the Dorset village quick enough. He was longing to see Liz: to make love to her: tell her of his plans to take her to Scotland: to make her rich and show her the diamonds. He also thought that the village would be the ideal place to stay out of the way for a while.

CHAPTER FOUR

Howard Hartwell soon began to feel chilled to the bone standing on the almost deserted platform of the small Staffordshire Station, the cold January night air penetrating even his usually warm overcoat. The north-easterly wind blew gustily across the line causing the few travellers waiting for the train to sink their heads into their shoulders, and curl up like snails crawling into their shells. Except for the wind, there was an eerie quietness about the place as the people sat on the cold hard seats which were spaced out along the platform. The powerful express trains frequently made a brief stop at this lonely and desolate place in the Midlands, due to it being one of the few junctions where the Northern line crossed at right angles over and above this main route to Scotland from London's Euston Station.

Howard knew that the train journey that he was about to undertake would take up many hours of tedious travelling, with the same types of boring people who had been on the train on every occasion previously. He usually found that his fellow travellers were not the best conversationalists, and on a long journey he would often fall asleep for most of the way. There would be the polite, 'thank you' or 'excuse me', with the odd 'sorry' thrown in now and again: most appeared to resent their privacy being disturbed, even in a crowded compartment. Howard always took a book to read, and one that he had already read or was in the middle of reading, as he found that these were easiest to concentrate on. Combined with the rhythmic sounds of steel wheels of the carriages passing over the rail joints and junctions, reading often helped to lull him off to sleep.

He looked at his watch which confirmed that the express was now almost three-quarters of an hour behind its scheduled time. It wasn't unusual for trains to arrive at Glasgow's Central Station up to one and a half hours late, and, because of this, he always caught this earlier train. After arriving in Glasgow, he would then get aboard one of the covered wagons which would be waiting to take him and others to the Naval Air Station at Abbotsinch. If there was no transport sent from the camp, they would need to catch the bus or tram from just outside the station to Paisley. From there it was another mile-and-a-half walk to the Naval Air Station where Howard was serving his time as an Air Mechanic in the Fleet Air Arm.

He had only been late back on one previous occasion, when he had caught a later train hoping that it would be on time, only for it to be held up at Carlisle for over an hour. He eventually arrived in Glasgow two and a half hours adrift. Fortunately, a Sub-Lieutenant and a young Wren Officer who had been travelling together on the same train, had seen Howard's hat band with 'HMS Sanderling' on it, noticed his worried look, and taken pity on him by taking him to breakfast at a nearby cafe. The officers had then accompanied him through the gates at the camp without a word being said by the guard on duty about him being over two hours late. He glared at Howard as he went through with a superior air, and on future occasions that same guard always gave him a puzzled look, as if trying to discover what influence he must have had on the two officers who had been with him on that morning, and prevented him from being 'put on a charge' for being adrift. If he had asked, Howard had been ready with his answer that his father was an admiral in the navy, but he was sorry that he never had the opportunity to be able to perpetrate that lie.

Five more long minutes went by, before the huge engine pulling the twelve coaches, screeched and squealed to a halt amidst clouds of steam and white smoke which almost blocked out the doors and windows of the carriages. Doors suddenly clattered open, there was shouting and, seconds later, more loud banging as doors clicked back to their original locked positions, a whistle blew and the train jerked violently, nearly knocking Howard off his feet as he moved down the corridor.

He had to stoop a little to enable him to peer into each badly-lit compartment looking for one with plenty of room, but most had three or four of those usual boring-looking people on each side, either staring out of the window, sleeping, or reading books or newspapers. Howard smiled to himself when he saw no-one having a conversation of any kind, confirming his theory that most people lost their ability to speak when travelling. He amused himself with the thought that being English, perhaps they didn't converse because they hadn't been introduced! He had almost decided to squeeze in between two fat ladies, one of whom was knitting a scarf which appeared to be already four or five feet long, when he noticed that the next compartment's blinds were down.

Hesitating for a moment to decide whether to try the door, he made a noise as if falling against it before sliding it partly open. This he thought would warn whoever was inside to stop whatever they were doing - if anything - as he reasoned it highly unlikely that the compartment was full of people. Surely they would hardly have all agreed to the blinds being pulled down if it had been.

He saw immediately there was only one seat occupied, and that by a very attractive girl sitting by the window. She turned to smile as he entered, but then looked disappointed, making it obvious that he wasn't the person she had expected to see come into the compartment.

"Is this anyone's seat?" Howard asked, pointing to the place opposite to where she was sitting. He knew immediately that it had been a stupid question as no one else was in the compartment, and he could see that, apart from a couple of suitcases on the rack, there was no other luggage, but he had to say something, and it had been the first thing that had come into his head.

The girl hesitated for a second before answering. "Er, no," and gave Howard another brief smile.

She was dressed very smartly in a plain fawn skirt, white jumper, and a heavy coat which was draped casually over her shoulders. She had one very shapely leg gently resting over the other, her skirt discreetly covering her knee. Howard immediately thought it odd that she wore sheer nylon stockings, as he knew that they were almost impossible to obtain throughout the war years, and still even now in 1945 when it looked as if the end of the war was in sight. Everyone knew that American soldiers could obtain them very easily, and with uncharitable suspicion, he believed that the G.Is gave them to our girls in exchange for services rendered. Howard dismissed the thought as being unkind, convinced that this beautiful girl could not possibly be guilty of that. He didn't want to spoil the excitement that he felt, and the luck he had had to find this lonely and lovely travelling companion. He wondered whom she had expected to see when he had walked in. Perhaps her mother or another female friend. But why the blinds down? Was she really alone, and who was her travelling companion? Howard noticed two cases on the rack, but could they both be hers?

The girl was idly flicking through the pages of a "Picture Post" she was holding, and, as the train picked up speed, she began rocking gently with the movement, her hair lightly brushing her cheeks in unison with the turning of the leaves of her magazine. Would she be going all the way to Glasgow as he hoped? He had to ask her to find out.

At that precise moment the door quickly slid open with a loud thump. The girl came suddenly alive, put down her book and greeted the tall good-looking American G.I. who had entered.

"You've been a long time, Joe." She gave him a broad smile, then surprised Howard by adding, "We've got company." She turned to look at Howard, giving him that same warm smile.

"Hi, fella. I'm Joe," the tall American said, with a huge grin and holding out his large hand towards Howard.

Howard introduced himself, half getting up off his seat, and shook the American's hand.

The G.I. looked back at the girl, and then went very serious for a second, shaking his head almost imperceptibly as he sat down.

"No-one," he said quietly.

"How far yer goin', fella?" he asked, returning to that same cheerful, bouncy attitude he had shown when he came into the compartment.

"All the way to Glasgow I'm afraid," Howard replied almost apologetically. He immediately wished he hadn't said it quite like that, as it must have sounded as if he was apologising for coming into the compartment. He was disappointed, however, as he had hoped that the girl's companion would have been female. It would have to be a man - and an American at that, he thought. Damn it!

Joe laughed. "Yer needn't be afraid, Howard, we ain't goin' to hurt yer," and he laughed again. "Here, have some candy." He threw Howard a bar of chocolate from out of his pocket.

Howard had put his case on the rack but kept hold of the book he had been carrying before boarding the train. He opened it and began to read. He was disturbed by the couple whispering quietly, and occasionally he caught a word or two of what they were saying. They both appeared to be worried about something at first, and then sat in silence for a while, before becoming more relaxed, and having a more pleasant conversation with each other. Howard couldn't concentrate, reading each page over and over again, before eventually settling down to become absorbed in his book.

Soon they were at Crewe, and then later, after reading a few more chapters, Howard noticed that they had arrived at Preston. He slept after that until he awoke to find that the train was almost in Carlisle.

He had begun to stir just before the train stopped, probably being disturbed by his two fellow passengers talking in loud whispers, apparently getting annoyed with each other again, and obviously disagreeing on something. Howard knew that this was going to be a much longer stop as the train always divided here with the front part of the train going on to Glasgow. The rear coaches would be coupled to one of the two engines of the train which would then proceed to Edinburgh. The announcement was repeated many times by the guard as he moved along the corridor to each compartment to ensure that everyone was aware of what was happening, and that the passengers were in the appropriate part of the train.

"No, no. You mustn't go," the girl was saying as she tugged at the sleeve of Joe's tunic, but the G.I. was insisting that he was going to leave the train temporarily and that there was nothing to worry about. Howard couldn't help wondering what it was all about. However, Joe was gone a long time, and the girl began to fidget, continually looking out of the window into the semi-darkness all the while he was away.

There appeared to be a lot of commotion and noise outside, and a small crowd of people on the platform were standing still, peering through the darkness towards the front of the train. Suddenly there were loud whistles, the train jerked, and then began to move forward very slowly. The girl jumped up in alarm and looked at Howard as if asking for help, her eyes wide open like a frightened animal.

"Joe's not back on the train!" she remarked almost hysterically, as she looked up towards the communication cord above the window. Howard jumped out of his seat to grab hold of her arm

29

before she could pull the red chain down which would apply the brakes to stop the train.

"NO! I'm sure there's no need. He will have got on at the last minute and he'll walk into the...." Howard stopped what he was saying as they both stared out of the window to the scene outside.

An American soldier was being led away by two U.S Military Police. They held him tightly by the arms, and Liz could just see his face in the semi-darkness of the platform. As the train crawled slowly by, Howard and the girl stood motionless for the few seconds it took for them to take it all in.

"That was Joe," she said, partly under her breath, and put her hand to her mouth after inhaling loudly.

Instinctively, Howard started to raise his own arm to reach for the communication cord, but she grabbed it as he had done hers only seconds before.

"No!" she gasped, as she appeared to lose all the air from her body, then collapsed lifeless, the energy and vitality she had shown earlier leaving her.

"Why not?" Howard demanded, wanting an explanation. "Why won't you let me stop the train? Surely you want to be with him and his suitcase is here." Getting no response from the girl, he then added in a firm voice, "Don't you care what might happen to him?"

The girl straighten up a little, then, lifted her head, looked straight into Howard's face. "Please sit down, I think I need your help."

Howard sat back down on his seat opposite without taking his eyes off her. He didn't understand her attitude. Her eyes were clear, still beautiful but without a tear. Her lips were pressed tightly together, determined. He wondered in what way she wanted him to help her, and it was plain to Howard that her mind was working hard trying to solve her dilemma. They sat looking at each other for what seemed an eternity. Howard knew that as soon as he began asking questions he'd be involved with her problems: He recalled the whispered conversations she had had with the American - the arguments and sharp exchanges that had taken place, the worried look they both gave when he had first entered the carriage, and the concern she expressed when he insisted on leaving the train for a while, but never to return. As events had proved, she had been right to be concerned, but now, as she appealed for Howard's help, it appeared that she was almost indifferent to his arrest.

Had she known what might happen by foreseeing the danger? Were the protests she made when Joe left the train just for show so that Howard wouldn't suspect her implication if things had gone wrong? He was suddenly aware that he had been staring into space as he had contemplated those far-fetched possibilities. "Well, I think you had better tell me why you need my help," Howard said calmly.

"Now he's been arrested, I think that I'd better tell you the whole story. Joe was a deserter," she began. "He was wanted by the military police for other offences, but I don't know the details. He was very worried that he'd be caught, and I tried to warn him not to leave the train. We had seen Military Police on the platform at Euston, but he didn't seem bothered about them as he believed that they had not recognised him, otherwise, he said, they would have stopped him from getting on." She stopped talking and looked at Howard.

He waited for her to continue, but she remained silent. "And that's it?" he asked. "That's the full story? Where do I come in, and why do you want my help? Come on," he said, "There must be more to it than that. You must tell me everything if you want me to do something to help you." Howard then had a sudden thought. If the part about the Military Police was true, they must have known that he had been on the train, so why hadn't they come aboard to make enquiries or look for his suit-case, or anything else that he might have been carrying. The American had left his hat on the seat. Howard looked at it then jumped up and opened the carriage door which led into the corridor. He was just in time to see two American soldiers with white belts and cap bands entering the next but one compartment.

"I thought so. They're examining the train and they'll be asking questions."

The girl quickly put Joe's hat underneath her. "Quick, sit next to me and kiss me."

Howard didn't need to be asked twice. Whatever the reasons why she wanted no one to know that she had known Joe, he wasn't going to miss this opportunity. He took her in his arms and pressed his lips against hers. Her skin was soft and she smelt heavenly. Almost at once the door opened, and Howard pulled away from her, feigning surprise. It had been all too short an embrace.

The soldier stood in the doorway. "Excuse me, lady. We're trying to find where a G.I. was sitting before he got off the train at the last station. Did you see him?"

"You're the only American soldiers we've seen," the girl answered calmly.

"Those belong to you two?" he asked, looking up to the racks at the three suitcases.

She followed his eyes and replied that two belonged to her, and Howard said that the other one was his.

"Sorry, to have disturbed you," he said, closing the door.

Howard turned back to the girl. "I think that this is a good time for you to tell me your name, don't you?"

She took hold of his arms, trying to get out of his grip. "My name is Elizabeth Harrison, but everyone calls me Liz, and you can go back to your seat now." She tugged at Howard's arms but he continued to hold her.

"And what if those men suddenly return and find us opposite

each other? Won't that look suspicious?"

"Well, alright then, but sit where you are and behave yourself."

He did as she said, but kept hold of her hand. "Is this alright?" he asked lifting their clasped hands off the seat. She nodded.

"You were telling me that he's been arrested for being a deserter. Is that all there is to it?"

She turned her head away from him and looked out of the window. Howard could see her reflection and she was looking at his.

"I first met Joe," she began, "about six months before he went to France after the Allies invaded Normandy. We became very friendly, and he brought me presents: nylons, perfume, make-up, you know all those things that we can't get because of the war. I was flattered, and I was young, and I...we.."

"Had an affair," Howard suggested completing her sentence for her.

She nodded. "And then we knew that the build-up of troops and equipment around the New Forest meant that France would soon be invaded, well, I thought that I might never see him again, even though he said he would come back for me after the war. I suppose I was in love with him and thought that he loved me too." She looked down at her lap. "But after a while, I began to discover things about him which I didn't like."

"Such as?" Howard asked, trying to sound compassionate.

"His lies. He told me that he'd stolen most of the things he brought me; even boasted about it, but as I didn't want to get him into trouble I said nothing to anyone."

"I think I'm beginning to see why you don't want to get involved, but why do you need my help! Oh hell! I've just thought. If they check our tickets, they will notice that yours is from London and mine is from the Midlands. We'll have to be careful of what we say if they question us."

She suddenly let go Howard's hand and became frightened.

"Oh, I was forgetting....his case....we must empty his case and get rid of it."

"We can't do that. Those two Army Policemen will probably come back to make a more detailed search when they can't find out which compartment he was in. Remember they saw your cases on the rack, and you did say that both were yours!" Howard reminded her.

Her eyes were wide open and she looked scared.

"There's something you haven't told me," Howard said, "Why must we empty his case? Do you know what's in it?"

She went pale, and spoke very quietly. "A lot of money."

"Cash?"

"No, diamonds."

Howard put his fingers through his hair and closed his eyes, hoping to find that he had only been dreaming all this. "Oh my God!" he exclaimed. When he opened them again she was still there. "And I'd always imagined that it was only blondes that were dangerous," he added flippantly.

He then thought about what she had said. "We can't - we mustn't do anything about his case. If they come back after they discover that he hasn't been anywhere else on the train, they might suspect that we weren't telling the truth, and we have no one else in our compartment to back up our story that he wasn't here." Howard was trying in vain to think of an excuse they could give if they examined their luggage and found the diamonds.

Suddenly the door opened again and there stood the other Military Policeman.

"Are you sure you didn't see him?" he asked, looking at them both in turn. He asked the question much more authoritatively than his colleague had asked it the last time.

Howard suddenly felt very calm. "Perhaps he was in one of the other carriages that have gone to Edinburgh," he suggested.

"Sure. We've thought of that. We're checking that train as well."

As the door closed, Liz looked at Howard, her eyes and mouth wide open with incredulity. "How on earth did you think of that?"

"Never mind," Howard said seriously. "What I want to know is what happened when you met Joe again?" He began to suspect that she was being deliberately evasive.

The girl looked at him for a while before answering his question, wondering how much to tell him. She dropped her eyes and looked down into her lap. "I suppose I'd better tell you the whole story," she began. "When I saw Joe being taken away, the thought went through my mind that I would be able to make myself a fortune, but I think I now realise that there's no way that I'll be able to handle this all by myself."

She lifted her head to look at Howard again, but he was already feeling somewhat apprehensive at offering to help her now that he was hearing about the way she was thinking. He knew that to do so, would mean inevitably that he would become involved in something that sounded very dangerous.

"Joe came back in December," she continued, "and at first it seemed quite normal that he had come back to England on leave, but then he told me what he'd done."

"Had he had stolen the diamonds from a house or bank that had been bombed?" Howard asked, allowing her the opportunity to give a plausible explanation.

"Worse than that." Her voice began to break, and Howard thought she was going to cry. "He told me that he'd robbed a jeweller in Belgium and had to kill him as he went to sound the alarm. He told me a long story of how he came back on a hospital ship with the wounded, but I didn't take much notice of what he was saying as I was thinking all the while what a terrible thing he had done." She paused, and then added, "Then he showed me the diamonds, and I forgot about that poor Belgian."

"He was wanted for murder then?" Howard said, stating the obvious. "I would have thought that there's no doubt that the

Military Police were waiting for him at Carlisle to arrest him for it. I expect that they also knew about the diamonds, but, if that was the case, I wonder why they didn't search the train before it left Carlisle? And then again, if they didn't know what he was carrying, they possibly didn't know about the murder, so perhaps they have arrested him only for desertion after all. There seems to be a lot of questions requiring an answer," he considered.

"I wouldn't have thought that just looking for his luggage was important enough to stop the train from leaving Carlisle," Liz observed, "but if they knew about the diamonds, I think that would have been, and they'd have searched the train until they found them. I believe that they were just trying to find out if anybody was travelling with him."

The girl's explanation sounded plausible to Howard, and would also seem to explain why the police had made their enquiries. They must have decided that Joe had been in one of the coaches that had gone to Edinburgh after all. However, when the two pairs of M.Ps contacted each other after the two trains arrived at their destinations, things might change very quickly.

"So what do we do with his case?" Howard asked, "leave it here or throw it out of the window?" He got up from his seat and began strutting about the carriage nervously. "Or perhaps we could hide it under the seat." As he sat down again he was beginning to feel scared of what might happen if it all went wrong.

Liz leaned forward and took hold of his hands and spoke very quietly. "Nobody knows the diamonds are here and I know where Joe was taking them. He was going to get a lot of money for them. What's to stop us from doing what he was going to do and keeping the cash for ourselves?"

Howard couldn't believe what she was saying. She appeared to be so cool about it all. It even looked as if she'd planned all this, only she couldn't have, surely?

"Do..you..know..what..you're..saying, Liz?" Howard's mouth

felt dry and his words came out staccato.

"Joe told me that there were almost 300 carats of diamonds in the packet, for which he had been offered about £50,000. Although he believed that it was far less than what they were worth, we could be rich if we shared it out between us," she said slowly and deliberately.

Blimey! What he couldn't do with £25,000!, Howard thought to himself, but what she was suggesting was preposterous. If the M.Ps did know about the diamonds, perhaps they would search all the luggage as the people left the train, which would reveal who was carrying them. As well as trying to find out if anyone had seen the American, they had also asked about the luggage. Even if they didn't know about the diamonds, they would surely want to know what was in his luggage if they could have found it. Howard had no doubts that the authorities in Carlisle would have already informed the police in both Glasgow and Edinburgh, and that someone would be waiting when the trains arrived at their destinations. There was no way that they would be able to get away with what this girl was suggesting. Howard dismissed any possibility of it succeeding.

"No one knows we have the diamonds," Liz said quietly as if reading his thoughts.

"How did you both get on the train at Euston?" Howard asked. "Someone must have seen you together." He didn't wait for her to answer but decided to tell her what he'd been thinking. "Perhaps the police do know that Joe was carrying diamonds, and you'll be caught red-handed when they look inside your cases. They purposely didn't inspect the luggage on the train, because if they had, you could have said you were innocent. That's it! They'll get you when you carry his case through the barrier." He knew now that it was impossible. "So there's no way we can get away with it," Howard concluded.

She was smiling at him. Why was she smiling he wondered?

What had he overlooked?

"Firstly," she began, "Joe deliberately waited until the very last minute before leaping on to the train as it was beginning to move. I was watching very carefully from my seat to make sure that nobody followed him. Secondly, he'd been very careful to ensure that we were not seen together on the platform, and thirdly, I'm not going to carry the case when we get off the train - you are!"

Now Howard was convinced that she was not as innocent as she was making out to be. She had planned this trip very carefully with Joe, and even had an important role to play herself. She was so obsessed with cashing in the illegal transaction that even Joe's arrest was not going to deter her from still carrying out the plans they had made. Indeed, it had made it easier for her. The only difference, Howard now began to realise, was that instead of Joe and her, it was going to be him and her. Howard looked into her beautiful face and saw a hardness for the first time. Her bright green eyes were now more dull in colour. They were cold calculating eyes. The sparkle had gone.

"First we can make sure that no one is waiting at the barrier and then we'll meet later." She paused and then added. "Just think, £25,000 for just carrying a case!" She gave him a lovely smile and squeezed his hand. Her eyes were sparkling again, but Howard's heart was thumping hard inside his chest, and he had sweat in the palms of his hands.

"There are some more sailors on the train going to your place, so if you went off with them no one would stop you," she told him firmly.

Howard shook his head in case he was dreaming. Perhaps he'd wake up from this nightmare. He looked up at the case on the rack. It wasn't dissimilar to his own. He could carry it under his overcoat in his other hand. Would it be that easy? He stood and took the case off the rack. It was surprisingly light. Without asking her he tried the catches, and surprisingly they sprang open.

Inside were items of Joe's personal possessions, underclothes and a shirt. There was also a bulging sealed envelope wrapped up in lots of tissue paper.

"The stones are in there," she said.

With the envelope in his hand containing the diamonds, and the £25,000 in his head, Howard now began to think more clearly. "I could carry these in the inside pocket of my overcoat, and you could take Joe's case off the train with yours. We could put Joe's possessions in my case, and you could put some of yours into his. Remember that you did tell those M.Ps. that they were both your cases, and if they should see you with only one, they'll wonder what happened to the other."

With the exchanges complete, Howard closed up the case and returned it to the rack, then sat back in his seat contemplating the situation. "Do you think it'll work?" he said tentatively.

"I'm certain," she said clearly and calmly.

Howard still felt some panic, but she looked very cool, he thought, but then why shouldn't she? - she wouldn't be carrying the diamonds!

"When will you be able to get away to meet me?" she asked.

He told her that he didn't know exactly, but usually it was easy enough to get a pass-out in the evenings. He would obviously be giving her the diamonds outside the railway station, but how did he know that he would ever see her again? How could he guarantee that she would wouldn't just disappear afterwards?

"Arrangements have been made to meet the dealer next Wednesday, but I think that it will be too risky for you to give me the diamonds after we leave the train," she explained as if recognising his fears. "You'd better keep them, and I'll contact you later when I've found out that everything is okay to go ahead."

"But I thought that I was only just going to...."Howard began. Liz interrupted him by putting a finger to her lips. "Ssh! don't change things now. It will work as long as we keep to the plans we've made."

"Where will you stay?" he asked, being worried in case she didn't get in touch with him again for some reason.

"Oh that was all arranged by Joe. It's a small hotel in St.Enoch's Square, but I'll have to make some excuse for his absence when I get there."

It all seemed very complicated to Howard, but Liz sounded confident that she could deal with it, so he asked no more questions. Nothing else was said for a long time as the train sped on its way to its destination. They both stared out of the window watching the pale orange sunrise on the distant horizon, suddenly to disappear behind the dark grey rolling hills of the Scottish Lowlands, and blend with the valleys and deep shadows of this changing landscape.

Howard felt exhausted, not only through lack of sleep but because all the events of the night had sapped his energies. He looked across to where Liz was sitting, her eyes closed trying to catch a few moments of sleep before the train reached its destination. She looked beautiful. If only all this hadn't happened, he could easily have fallen in love with her. She was obviously a girl with passions, and he fantasized about making love to her before he too fell into a light sleep.

They awoke at about the same time, and Howard put the blinds back up on the corridor windows to make it appear that they were just ordinary passengers, and not accomplices of a diamond smuggler and murderer, (even though the real criminal had been arrested). Howard reminded himself that he was now also the receiver of stolen goods, and even when he had given them back to Liz and received the large sum of money he had been promised, he knew that he would still think of himself as a criminal, albeit a wealthy one.

As soon as the train began to slow down, they deliberately

made quite a show of their parting for the benefit of anyone watching. They kissed in the corridor and shouted their goodbyes loudly, before Howard put his head out of the window to watch the train sliding into the station alongside the platform. No one was waiting at the barriers except a solitary railway official.

Howard jumped off the train almost before it had stopped and hurried towards the barrier, carrying his own small attache case and wearing his overcoat buttoned up tightly around him. He joined up with the other servicemen, including sailors from his camp, and hurried past the ticket collector handing him his ticket. Howard glanced back and saw the two M.Ps running along the platform to the barrier, but he was through before they reached it.

He looked up at the station clock and saw that the train had arrived over an hour late. All the Navy personnel were rushing to get outside where a truck was waiting to take them to the Naval Air Station at Abbotsinch. Moments later in the cold, raw air of that early hour, they were trundling along the empty road to Paisley, seated on the wooden benches in the covered wagon. Howard felt nervous, aware of the bulge in the inside pocket of his overcoat, knowing that he would not be happy until he had actually arrived safely in the camp, and able to put the package away and out of sight.

CHAPTER FIVE

Over the week-end Howard scanned the newspapers in the library on the camp to find a report of the arrest at Carlisle Station, and what might have happened to the American, but there was none. He concluded that it had not been worth a news item, as it was commonplace for soldiers to be arrested for being absent without leave, and in any case, the papers were full of the latest news of the war in Europe.

On Tuesday afternoon, he received word from a colleague that there was a girl at the guard house asking to see him. His informant described her lovely red hair which left him in no doubt who she was. He had just returned from the hangars on the other side of the airfield, and by five o'clock he had obtained leave to go 'Ashore' for twelve hours. Actually, this took effect straight away but he had to be back in camp by 8 a.m. next morning. After sending her a message, he met Liz in the cafe in the High Street. She greeted him with a sweet smile. He had the brown envelope containing the diamonds safely tucked away in the inside pocket of his overcoat.

"Have you had a look inside?" she asked as he handed it to her.

From the look he gave her she could tell immediately that he hadn't even opened the package, but Howard was more interested to know what had happened at Central Station after he had left, or whether perhaps she had heard from Joe. He remained silent as the waitress brought the pot of tea which Liz must have ordered as soon as she saw him coming. Howard noticed that she too had ginger hair, and the whole of her pretty face completely covered in freckles. She would have been only a few years younger than the girl sitting opposite him, but compared with her she looked so innocent, and Howard guessed that her life wasn't anywhere near as complicated as Liz's.

"Did they search your luggage?" he asked anxiously when the young girl had left.

"There were a number of soldiers including two G.I's that they took to one side, but I don't know what happened to them. The two Military Policemen that we saw on the train, questioned some of the other passengers, but I don't think they examined any of the suitcases people were carrying. When it came to my turn they just smiled at me, asked about you, then said what a lucky fella' you were."

Howard laughed, and thought if only they knew how accurate their comments had been.

"But I have something else to tell you which is worrying," Liz continued, "and it's also why I haven't contacted you earlier."

Howard waited anxiously for what she was about to say. She paused, appearing to try and find the right way to tell him what was concerning her.

"I've found something out about Joe's accomplice, although I don't know a lot about him, or whether he has any knowledge of the package.

"How do you know? I mean how did you find out?"

"I went to the hotel in St.Enoch's Square where Joe had said he had booked a room. When I got there I found that they were expecting a Mr. and Mrs. Harrison on honeymoon! Harrison is my name. Apparently, the room had been booked in December by a soldier with the name, McKern, but it seems that no mention had been made that Joe was an American G.I."

"And how are you going to explain it when he doesn't turn up? and how do you know that he won't? I've been worrying about that." Howard sounded concerned.

Liz looked down at the tablecloth and paused before answering. "I don't believe he will turn up now. I talked to a British Officer who's in the hotel about what happens to deserters, and he told me that the army treats the offence very seriously. I'm certain that he won't be around for some time, and will probably be sent back to America." Then she lifted her eyes and stared into his. "To answer your first question, I told them that my husband was in the Royal Navy."

Howard's mouth dropped open. He had hardly taken any notice of what she had said about Joe, and couldn't decide at first whether she was referring to himself when she had said that her husband was in the Navy, or had just made up a plausible explanation to the hotel management. "What do we do now?" he asked innocently, ignoring the implications of her remark. She gave him a broad smile and he thought how beautiful she looked. Her skin was smooth and without a blemish, her eyes sparkled, and she had just the right amount of lipstick to complement the colouring of her lovely groomed red hair. Howard knew that he would have gone along with whatever she suggested at that point, but what she said next still took him by surprise.

"Will you come back to the hotel with me now. I believe that they are beginning to think that I haven't got a husband."

"You haven't," he said, raising his eyebrows, and then suddenly fearing that he might have lost an opportunity added, "but you don't have to ask twice for me to act like one."

She reached across the table and took his hand into hers. A gentle hand, warm and soft. She was looking at him with those clear green eyes. He dared not ask what he hoped was on her mind. It was certainly on his. But then he thought about Joe's accomplice.

"What about..."

Liz stopped him in mid-sentence. "I know what you are going

to ask, but that's why I waited a while before contacting you. If that man had travelled on our train, he couldn't possibly have known what we had planned and, what's more, he would also have seen Joe arrested. He would then have either looked for me on the train or in the hotel knowing that Joe wouldn't turn up. He didn't, so I don't think he's here. My belief is that Joe befriended him on the hospital ship, and gave him some money just to book the room in the hotel."

"You seem to have worked it out well and thought of everything, Liz." Howard's worries were over. He had given her the diamonds, and now all he could think of at this moment was that he was going to spend the evening with her.

She leant forward and spoke in a very quiet voice, "But I'm afraid I do have a disappointment for you...."

He knew it. He thought it too good to be true, then suddenly he remembered the way she had pushed him away in the railway carriage after he had kissed her. She used him then, and now she was going to use him again.

"The porter gave me a letter this morning addressed to Mr.Harrison. He'd had it for some time. I read it. It was from the jeweller..."

She looked quickly about her to see if anyone was listening to their conversation, but the few other ladies in the cafe - Howard was the only man - were all busy concentrating on their own small talk. Perhaps there wasn't going to be any money in it for him after all. It had all been a ruse on her part to get him to take the diamonds off the train. He waited for the punch line.

"...he has reduced his offer to £40,000," she continued, "so that's only twenty thousand each instead of twenty-five."

Howard's eyes opened wide and he didn't know what to say. Only £20,000 she had said. £20,000! Oh, my God, he thought, who cares? I'll still be rich.

"He also confirmed that it is tomorrow night when we see him.

At eight o'clock he will have taken them off our hands. Meanwhile, you can have a bonus and we'll celebrate our good fortune." She had chosen that word "celebrate" deliberately, remembering what Joe used to mean when he said it.

Although that was something to look forward to, in whatever form it would take, Howard suddenly felt very nervous about taking the American's place; perspiration was beginning to form on his brow, and the palms of his hands were sweating. He wasn't really listening to what else Liz was saying, but she had just mentioned something about him collecting his bonus.

"A bonus?" he asked. "What do you mean, a bonus?"

"You've earned it, Howard." She was smiling at him. "You don't have to be back until morning do you?"

Liz noticed that his cheeks had turned a bright red, and as they left the cafe Howard couldn't remember whether he had finished his tea or not. Cis and Lil, two well known prostitutes of uncertain age, were standing at the corner close to the bus stop. They never took their eyes off Howard's beautiful companion as they walked by, then laughed together at their own private joke. He had previously felt a little envious of some of the lads at the camp who had been out with them, but now he thought how repulsive they both were. Paisley also had a profusion of pretty girls mostly employed at the local textile factory, but he knew that he had the most beautiful girl in the world at his side.

The bus seemed to take an interminable length of time to arrive in Glasgow, picking up at every stopping place on the journey. When they eventually arrived at the hotel, Liz slipped her arm through Howard's as they approached the reception desk. After she gave her room number, the clerk handed her the key and greeted Howard with a cheery, "Good evening, Mr. Hartwell."

Howard was taken completely by surprise. "How did he know my name?" he asked, as they walked away from the desk.

"I told you that the Scotsman had booked the room in my name, but I changed it to yours. It was fortunate that he had kept Joe's identity a secret," she said, as they approached the lift. "You must be pleased that you haven't had to hire a G.I's uniform and put on an American accent." She laughed, then added, "Aren't you lucky?"

Howard certainly had to agree to that, but for a completely different reason from the one she had given.

An hour or so later they had a wonderful romantic meal in the restaurant, drank a bottle of Bollinger 1935 - which the waiter explained had been brought by the soldier when he booked the room (no doubt another of Joe's thefts he'd brought back from France, Liz guessed, and a companion to the other one they had shared when Joe first showed her the diamonds). They followed this with a couple of glasses of Scotch which the hotel had somehow conjured up, no doubt because they thought that they were on their honeymoon. The knowing smile they received from the head waiter as they left the dining room also confirmed what the misinformed staff must have been thinking. The thought went through Howard's mind that the cost of the meal didn't matter; he would have plenty of money to pay the hotel bill tomorrow.

Next morning he awoke early to find himself in the most luxurious bed he had ever slept in, lying with the most beautiful girl he could ever have dreamed about, naked by his side. He wanted to make love to her again there and then, but knew that the clock prevented him from doing so. Their clothes were scattered all over the floor, and Howard smiled when he remembered the trouble that they both had had trying to remove his uniform the night before. The tight fitting 'top' of the 'square rig' traditional Navy uniform was always difficult to remove in normal circumstances, but after all that alcohol, and the desire to remove their clothes urgently, had caused all sorts of problems, until eventually they had both ended up practically in hysterics.

The smile left his face as he looked again at his watch, realising that he had just enough time to get back to the camp. It was almost six-thirty. It would take him about an hour to get back after leaving the hotel, and he knew that if Liz woke up he would never be able to get back on time. So he slipped out of bed quietly, dressed hurriedly, then woke his 'newly wed wife' to say goodbye.

"Thanks for the bonus," he whispered. "I'll see you here as quickly as I can tomorrow, and after we've met this contact of yours, do I get more bonuses?" he asked flippantly.

"If you're a good boy," she said, flinging her arms around his neck, kissing him passionately.

Howard dragged himself away telling her reluctantly that there was no time. "I must go, and if I'm late I won't be able to get leave tomorrow." He left the room hurriedly not daring to look back.

The day seemed interminably long, and Howard couldn't stop thinking about the night before. The diamonds were now only his second thought. He didn't care if they only got a few pounds for them. The thrill of being with her was enough. He still wasn't happy about meeting this dealer or diamond merchant whoever he was. He must surely have been a crook, and Howard worried about the risk they were going to take. He also didn't know anything about diamonds, but it seemed strange that the price had apparently been agreed without the buyer never having seen the goods. After they had received the money in exchange for the diamonds, would he ever see her again? Would the payment be in cash, and how would he explain his own sudden rise to riches? The Scottish soldier she had talked about also worried him. Where was he? Had he been paid by Joe for making the arrangements, and what else did he know? Howard pushed all of these questions to the back of his mind. He just wanted to feel her warm body next to his and make love to her again.

He left the camp about five o'clock and arrived at the hotel about an hour later.

She was waiting in her room and appeared a little nervous.

"I've looked at the diamonds. They're beautiful," she said. "I just had to open the package and I've taken the two biggest ones out."

She passed one over to Howard. "Here - one each. I don't think the jeweller will notice as his offer is way below the real price he should be paying for them."

"What are we going to do?" Howard asked. "We have a lot of time to spare." He wanted to make love to her.

"Let's eat," she suggested.

Howard felt a pang of disappointment, but they had the whole night ahead of them, and they'd have no time for eating when they had the money in their possession. He began to fantasise about making love to her with five-pound notes strewn all over the bed.

They ordered the best meal on the sparse menu, starting with game soup, followed by poached salmon and Hollandaise sauce, and baked apple for sweet. As there was no wine obtainable, they drank a couple of large gin and tonics with their meal.

"I think it's time we left," Howard suggested as he looked at the clock in the restaurant. It was showing twenty minutes to eight. "Hope you've got the package safe?" he said, smiling at Liz. Howard thought that she looked particularly ravishing. He called the waiter and signed the bill. It looked like a lot of money for a meal for just two people; more than he was paid in a month in the Navy, but he didn't care. Money didn't matter.

They walked out of the hotel and through St. Enoch's Square into Union Street, then continued along Renfield Street. It was a cold night, and the wind cut right through their outer garments as they approached Sauchiehall Street. It had taken them longer than they thought, the clocks having struck eight o'clock long before they had reached the tiny premises of the jeweller's shop. It was very dark; the street lamps dimmed due to the blackout still being in force. There was a sinister atmosphere about the area as they went round the corner of a little side street to knock on the back door of the building. It was fortunate that Liz had already been in the daylight to find out exactly where it was - they would never had found it in the dark if she hadn't. Howard knocked a little louder the second time when no one came.

"Who's there?" It was a man's voice and the question was asked in a very cautious manner.

"Elizabeth Harrison. You're expecting me."

They heard the bolts on the other side of the door sliding back and then the click as the locks were released. The door opened and the a small, slightly bent old man in his late sixties greeted her. "Come in. I have been expecting you," and then, peering at Howard in the darkness, he asked, "Who's this?" He sounded concerned.

"Oh it's alright," Liz assured him, "he's a friend."

"I heard about Joe," the old man said suddenly as he closed the door behind them.

"How did you know?" Howard asked. He was sure that there had been no publicity.

"The soldier who brought me the diamonds on Saturday told me."

"Brought you the diamonds!?" they said together.

The old man noticed their expressions, wondering why they seemed surprised. "The fellow said that it was lucky that he had been given the diamonds as Joe feared that something might happen to him on his journey to Scotland, but that you would be coming as arranged to see me. I wrote to Joe at the hotel last week, but as Joe isn't here perhaps you read the letter."

Liz looked puzzled and Howard tried to clarify the situation. "You mean that the soldier had said that Elizabeth would be coming for the money that Joe should have had?" Howard asked.

"No! I gave him the money when he showed me the diamonds. You seemed surprised. He said that you knew all about it and would be coming to thank me."

"But I have Joe's diamonds here," Liz said, handing the old man the packet she took from her handbag.

Nothing was said as the old man opened the packet and tipped out the diamonds onto a black velvet cloth lying on the table. They glittered and shone in the light of a powerful lamp which the old man had switched on to examine the stones, his eye-glass pressed tightly into his right eye socket. He went quickly from one stone to another as he examined them, his face expressionless. "Fakes," he said, putting the eye-glass back on the table, "completely worthless". You might get ten pounds for them if you're lucky to be sold as costume jewellery."

Liz put her hands to her face as she took a deep breath. Howard wanted to laugh but wondered how Liz would react if he did.

The old man looked at the girl. "Where did you get them?"

Howard could see that Liz was in state of shock so he answered for her. "Joe was bringing them to Scotland with Elizabeth. She thought that they were the real thing," Howard explained. "Do you know where this Scotsman is, by the way?" Howard tried to make it sound as if the question was quite normal in the circumstances.

The old man shrugged his shoulders, and assured them that he knew nothing of the soldier's whereabouts. Liz looked as if she was going to explode. Her face was red and her mouth open as if she was about to speak, but no words came.

"Are you sure about this?" Howard asked, trying to remain as calm as possible: more for Elizabeth's sake than his own. "Could you not have made a mistake?" he asked again.

"There's no doubt, I'm afraid, no doubt at all."

Howard thought that the old man appeared uncomfortable and noticed that he was giving Liz a pitiful look. "I could give you ten pounds for them," he announced suddenly.

Howard hoped that had been his first offer. "Can't you make it any more?"

The old man scratched his wrinkled chin, and looked again

sympathetically at Howard's shattered companion, "Well, I suppose I could go to £12, but that's my last offer."

Liz found her voice. "Take it. Let's get out of here." She sounded very angry. As they walked back to the hotel, Liz was in a lousy mood. She was at a loss to understand how it had happened and cursed Joe for his deceit.

"I'm glad he got arrested," she said without showing any feeling of remorse." He was a liar and a...a....." she couldn't find the right words and started to cry.

There was only one explanation in Howard's mind as to what had gone wrong. Joe must have made friends with this Scotsman, told him about the diamonds, and asked him to make arrangements for the trip to Glasgow. It was almost certain that he also knew about the dealer in Sauchiehall Street where the stones could be sold safely, Howard reasoned. It must have been after that when the Scotsman stole them, and somehow replacing them with the fake ones without Joe knowing. Joe could not have known about the switch of the stones, otherwise he would not have gone to all that trouble just to bring them to Scotland. He must have thought that the real ones were in his case.

Howard told Liz all of this but it didn't help.

The wind was much colder now and Howard's legs felt heavy. The journey back seemed twice as long as when they came. Liz looked as if she was going to fall over on a number of occasions but rejected Howard's offers to help each time.

They went immediately to their room at the hotel feeling very cold and dejected. The bed looked less inviting now, but, perhaps in a little while when she had overcome her disappointment, things might be a little different. They could still have a wonderful night together, Howard thought, but he saw that she was packing her case in a hurry, throwing her things in as quickly as she could and sobbing as she did so. Then she was gone without even saying goodbye.

CHAPTER SIX

Howard sat on the bed feeling empty and at a loss as to what to do next. But what had he lost? Nothing really. Nothing that he didn't have previously. Then an awful thought struck him - he suddenly realised that he had a huge hotel bill to pay, and no money! Liz had kept the small amount she had received from the jeweller, and although he had thought jokingly at the time to ask her for half of it, he really had not had the heart to mention it again. He felt into his pocket and took out what little money he had. At least he had enough to buy a couple of drinks or so. Among the coins, he saw the now worthless diamond that Liz had given him, believing it to be the genuine thing at the time. It was shining almost in defiance at its minute value. It looked so real as it glistened, reflecting the lights of the room.

Howard suddenly had a hair-brained idea. Would he be able to get away with offering it to the hotel in payment of the bill by pretending it to be the real thing? He would be prepared to accept far less than its apparent value, but just what value should he put on it? First he must find out what the hotel bill was going to be, then he could decide. If one of the management could tell it was not a real diamond, he would plead ignorance and tell them that he had been cheated by the lady who had given it to him, and who they thought to have been his wife. It would be most embarrassing for him to admit that they had used the hotel for an affair, but it was the only thing that he could think of. If he left without paying, the hotel already had his name, and would soon be able to trace him at the Naval Air Station at Abbotsinch, so he really had no alternative but to try something, and that was all he had.

Howard went downstairs, walked boldly to the bar, and was immediately greeted by the barman.

"Good evening, Mr.Hartwell," he said cheerily, "wife not with you?"

Howard was taken a little by surprise and wondered how to answer. He thought that the truth would be best. One lie would only lead to another.

"Gone back, I'm afraid. Could I have a half-a-pint of bitter and a chaser please?" He hoped that the barman would not go into the matter further. Howard moved away from the bar immediately he had been served, carrying his glass of beer and his tot of scotch, and sat down on his own. He began to have misgivings about what he had planned to do. Would he really be able to get away with it? Even if he did, when they discovered the truth they would still be able to find him, and then he could be in very serious trouble, with both the Naval authorities and, no doubt, the police too!

After thinking hard about the situation, he decided to tackle the problem immediately rather than wait until the next day. In any case, he wouldn't be able to sleep for thinking about what might happen in the morning. The drink had given him courage as he went to the reception desk and told the porter that his wife had had to go back to London earlier than they had planned, but she had, unfortunately, taken all their money with her. He said that he was wondering how much he owed, because he was concerned about not having enough money to pay the bill immediately, unless he could get some cash the next day.

He was pleased that the porter didn't ask him to explain what he had meant by his last remark, but went away to return a few minutes later with his account. Howard couldn't believe his eyes. "Oh, that much?" was all that he was able to say.

"You will see that it includes bed for tonight and breakfast tomorrow morning for both of you," the porter explained.

"Oh in that case, as I will be the only one here tonight," Howard said, "and will be leaving before breakfast, I wonder if these items could be deducted?"

"I can reduce the bill by charging for only one tonight, sir, but breakfast is included I'm afraid, whether you eat it or not."

It wouldn't make much difference, Howard thought, he still had to try to find the money. He boldly took the diamond from out of his pocket. "Would it be possible to try and find out how much this is worth and whether I could use it to pay the bill by any chance?" Howard tried to make his request sound as if it was quite the normal thing to have asked.

The porter looked at the diamond in Howard's hand then looked very seriously at Howard. It was very obvious that he'd never been asked before whether a hotel guest was able to pay the bill with anything other than a cheque or cash.

"I'll have to make enquiries, sir." Howard thought that he appeared to drawl out the 'sir' a bit longer than he normally did. He disappeared and was gone sometime. Meanwhile, Howard was left at the desk trying not to imagine the sort of conversation that was going on behind closed doors. After what appeared to be an interminable length of time, the porter emerged with the manager of the hotel close behind him.

"I understand that you are making enquiries as to whether you can pay you bill with a diamond, sir. Is that right?"

"Well, nearly right. You see my wife..."

"Yes, yes," the manager interrupted, "I fully understand the situation you find yourself in. The hotel porter has explained everything to me. I may be able to help. Fortunately we have staying in the hotel this evening a Mr.Klerk who is a jeweller whom I have already contacted. He will be down in a moment to value your diamond. If you would like to take a seat in the lounge,

I will bring him to you when he arrives."

Howard's heart sank. 'An expert in diamonds', he'd said! One glance and he would tell him what he already knew. He wondered whether he should leave now and hope that they wouldn't bother to try and find him. Howard heard voices, and he stood up to greet the diamond expert. He was a man in his middle-fifty's, short and stocky and not as tall as Howard; much overweight for his age, but looking extremely prosperous in his dark grey tweed suit. Howard didn't feel relaxed in spite of his warm smile and firm handshake.

"Please sit down, Mr er.."

"Hartwell," Howard said. Obviously the manager had not told him his name, or perhaps it was the man's way of relaxing his clients.

"I understand that you have a diamond requiring a value. Can I see it?"

Howard gave him the diamond, and even before he produced his eyeglass and put it to his eye, Howard expected him to say, "Rubbish!"

He examined it carefully but not for long. "Where did you get this. Mr Hartwell?"

"It was given to me as a present," Howard told him truthfully.

"You have a very fine stone here," he said. "I would quickly estimate it to be worth over a thousand pounds."

Howard could not believe his ears. "How much did you say?" he asked.

"I could be wrong," Mr. Klerk admitted, "It could be nearer two thousand than one. I'd need to examine it more carefully in better light and at length."

Howard tried to remain calm although he was sure that the man must have heard his heart beating hard against the wall of his chest. If only Liz was here he thought, but he remembered that she also had one which she had taken from out of the envelope. Was her's the same, or was this an odd one that had been mixed up with the others? Perhaps they had been all genuine diamonds and the fellow in Sauchiehall Street was in league with that soldier who he had told them about. He put all this out of his mind for the moment. The important thing was to sell the diamond before this fellow changed his mind.

"How much will you give me for it?" Howard asked. "I need to sell it urgently."

"Don't be in such a hurry, young man. You want to get the best price for it, and I'll try to do that if that is what you would like me to do."

Howard didn't want to wait that long. Even if this man had said it was worth more than he had originally valued, he would be satisfied with the thousand pounds. "I need to get back to the camp tonight," Howard lied. "Why can't you give me something for it now? I need the money urgently."

"How can I be sure that it is yours to sell?" the man asked calmly. "How do I know that you haven't stolen it, or whoever gave it to you didn't steal it? Forgive me for saying so, but it seems strange that someone should give you such a valuable diamond, and then you be prepared to accept less than its real value."

Howard didn't expect to be questioned like this, and he could almost see the police coming into the hotel to question him even more thoroughly. He began to wish that he had left it until the morning, taken it into one of the jeweller's shops in Glasgow, and then accepted what he would be offered for it. Some of them would be only too pleased to get a bargain. But of course, he hadn't known its worth until now. He thought that he could still do that tomorrow, but as he had to be back on the Station before 8am., he would have to come back in the evening. No, he needed to sell it now if he could. He decided to take a bold and more positive approach.

"If you don't want it, I'll sell it tomorrow for what I can get for it, and I'll just pay you the fee for valuing it for me," Howard told him. He noticed that Mr. Klerk suddenly looked a little disappointed.

"I didn't say that I didn't want it," he replied quickly. "Give me a little time to examine it more closely, and I'll make you an offer provided that you sign a guarantee that it is yours to sell."

"I'll do that willingly," Howard said. He had already worked it out that even if Liz discovered that her diamond was real too, there was no way that she would know whether his was real as well. Even if she returned to check if he still had the stone, who else could she tell about the diamonds? He could sign without any fear of anyone finding out where the diamond had come from. After all, the real thief, Joe the G.I., had been arrested.

The jeweller had moved to a small table with a bright table lamp and returned after thoroughly examining the stone.

"I'll give you eight-hundred-and-fifty pounds for it," he said firmly, immediately after he had sat down and handing the stone back to Howard.

Howard was impressed at the way that the jeweller had stated the figure he was prepared to give. There was no mistaking that it was a 'take it or leave it' offer, and no doubt the way that this fellow always conducted his negotiations in his business deals. There would be no point in haggling, Howard decided, so he accepted after a suitable, but only brief pause. Mr.Klerk produced a printed form from his inside pocket and called the Manager over to witness Howard's signature. Howard could see at a glance that it was an official document drawn up to ensure that Mr.Klerk or his company would be in the clear should any of his purchases prove to be stolen goods. Mr.Klerk wrote out the cheque, Howard gave him the diamond, they shook hands, and the jeweller left the room. With the agreement of the Manager of the hotel, Howard endorsed the cheque, paid his hotel bill, and pocketed the substantial balance.

Later that evening, after spending over ten shillings in the bar, Howard found it difficult to sleep for thinking about the soldier whom Joe had befriended and trusted. He would never know how the Scot had managed to get the diamonds from Joe.

He thought too about Liz, and began to feel sorry for her. She had been very disappointed after being told that the stones were not genuine, and he wondered where she had gone after she stormed out of the hotel.

CHAPTER SEVEN

Elizabeth Harrison had arrived at the Central Station just in time to board the overnight express to London. There was nothing else she could have done but to go back home with only the money that the jeweller had given her, and some of that she had used to buy her ticket.

She sat in a corner seat by the window of an empty compartment, and began to cry. She had set out with Joe less than a week ago with such high hopes of becoming rich, but so much had changed since that time. Firstly, Joe had been arrested and she didn't know what had happened to him since. Secondly, the diamonds he had been carrying had proved to be worthless, and thirdly, she had let down the only really decent man she had ever met in her life, by promising him half of the fortune she had hoped to make, only for him to finish with nothing. Indeed, he had been left to pay the hotel bill which she knew he couldn't afford. It saddened her to think that he didn't deserve that sort of treatment. She had cajoled him into helping her, and he had managed to get the diamonds off the train safely, agreeing with her demands all along the way. Even when they discovered that the diamonds weren't real he hadn't grumbled, although he must have been disappointed that he got nothing out of it after doing everything she had asked him to do. It was true that she'd let him make love to her but to leave him as she did was unforgivable. Thinking about Howard made her cry even more.

All the tension of the last few days had gone, and the

disappointment of returning home with nothing left her feeling dejected. She was tired and weak from all her crying, and this, together with the effect of the rhythm of the train on the rails, lulled her to sleep.

She awoke as the train jerked to a stop. It had reached Carlisle, and she found herself staring at the empty platform with an uncontrollable urge to try and find out what had really happened to Joe, and why he had left the train, especially as he knew that it might have been very risky to do so.

Carrying her case, she paraded up and down that same platform wondering if there might be someone she could ask who could remember the incident, and be able to give her some information. If they had found out that he was a murderer, she knew that she would never ever see him again. A porter saw her looking around and asked if he could help. Liz thought that there would be no harm in asking him a question or two.

"There was an American soldier who was arrested here last week," she said. "I was on the same train going to Scotland, and I wondered whether you knew why he had been arrested and what had happened to him."

The porter looked at her very seriously. "Did you know him, madam?" he asked.

Liz didn't quite know how to answer that question, and hesitated for a few seconds. The porter remained looking her: too intently she thought. "Well, I think he was the same American who I spoke to earlier on the train. He seemed such a nice person. I was only enquiring out of curiosity."

"Are you getting back on the train, madam?" the porter asked. "It'll be leaving very shortly if that is what you intend to do."

"I was wondering what time the next train to London is due, as I would like to stay here for a little while longer," Liz said, trying to sound very calm and in full control of herself.

"The London train from Edinburgh will be arriving in about an hour," the porter informed her in his official voice. "You'll be able to catch that one," and then surprised her by adding, "Still worried about that soldier, are you, madam?"

"Well, I would like to know - purely out of curiosity of course," Liz said again.

"Of course, madam. I'll go and make some enquiries for you." He walked very briskly away towards the Station Master's Office. Liz was beginning to wonder whether she ought not to continue with her enquiries and get back on the train, but it was too late! She remembered hearing the whistle blowing while she had been talking to the porter and, at that moment, she saw the train beginning to leave.

Liz sat down on one of the iron benches and waited for the porter to return. He was a long time, and she was beginning to feel very cold. She heard footsteps behind her and turned to see two policemen coming in her direction.

"Are you the lady that was asking about the American soldier who was arrested here last week?" the taller one asked politely. "I understand that you knew him."

"Well..er..no. Not really," Liz answered tentatively.

"We have reason to believe that you did." He now spoke with more authority in his voice, and then added, without waiting for Liz to reply, "I wonder whether you'd mind coming with us to the station, we would like to ask you some questions."

No-one spoke as she sat alone in the back seat of the police car on the way to the police station. She was pleased about that, as it gave her time to think. She wondered what she should admit to, and whether she should explain her relationship with Joe. What did they know about him? The authorities must have found out that he was a deserter, but did they know about the diamonds? What was more important, had they found out that he had murdered a Belgian civilian? They arrived at the police station much too quickly for her to be clear in her mind what she should do.

She was taken to a small room and sat facing a desk. Two plain clothes detectives came in and sat down facing her on the opposite side.

"Would you tell us who you are first," said the older of the two men, "and where you've been."

Liz gave them her full name and address, and told the men that she had travelled to Scotland with her boy friend who was in the Navy. She said that they had spent some time together and was now returning home. If they wanted to check on her story, she thought, they would find the last part to be true, as no one at the hotel in Glasgow had any knowledge of Joe. She felt satisfied that she had covered her tracks so far, so good.

"And why are you so interested in the U.S. soldier who was arrested on the station here in Carlisle?" the younger detective asked.

This was the question she had been dreading. She hesitated before answering, trying to find an answer which would sound plausible. Just to say that she was curious hadn't convinced the porter, and she knew it would be received with scepticism by the police.

The older man reached into a folder which was open in front of him, and took out a photograph which he slid across to her. "How long have you known this man?" he asked seriously.

Her eyes opened wide as she looked first at the photograph of the G.I., and then at the two detectives. "I've never seen this man before in my life," she answered truthfully. "Was this the man who was arrested?"

The older man leaned forward to look at Liz more closely. "Do you expect us to believe that you have never ever seen this man before?"

"You can believe what you like," Liz replied, now feeling more confident and relieved that it wasn't Joe that had been taken away by the Military Police. She was now anxious to clear this misunderstanding up very quickly as she wanted her mind to be clear to try to understand what had happened to Joe. At the same time, she didn't want them to know that she had been travelling with him because of the diamonds, so she explained to them that a G.I. who had been travelling in the same compartment as Howard and she, had introduced himself to them as Joe Peabody, and had got off the train at Carlisle. She told them that he had said that he would be back, but when they saw the American soldier being taken away, they assumed that it was this Joe they had met, and now, returning to London, she thought that she would try to find out why he had been arrested. "But this isn't Joe," she said, pointing to the photograph.

"So it was only curiosity that made you break your journey after all," the detectives remarked. "This Joe Peabody, did he not have a case with him or any other luggage?"

Liz had told one lie, and now she was about to tell another. If she gave them the right answer, she hoped that they wouldn't ask her any more questions. "No, I don't think that I recall him carrying anything."

The detectives looked puzzled. "Strange that he didn't return. And he didn't leave anything on the train?"

She had thrown the small attache case away that had originally contained the diamonds and Joe's things, and she now began to worry that it might have been found, and that the police were searching for the owner. She had to be careful how she answered. "Well, he might have been carrying a small case, but he certainly didn't leave anything on the train."

They asked a few more questions about Joe which she pretended not to know the answers to, repeating that they had met only on the train, and the detectives were finally convinced that Liz was telling the truth. "Perhaps you would give me the name of this boy friend of yours, as we might want to confirm your story:

purely routine you understand," they told her.

"Of course," Liz replied, and, after giving them what they wanted, asked, "Can I go now and catch the train to London? I hope I haven't missed it." She looked up at the clock and wondered whether she would be able to get back to the station in time.

"My sergeant will run you back, miss," said the older of the two men, "and thank you for your co-operation in this matter. If we need you again we have your address, but I doubt if it that will be necessary."

On the way to the station she quizzed the detective as to the identity of the American soldier, and the reason why he'd been arrested. He told her that he had been wanted for murdering a couple of black G.Is., and that the Military Police had seen him board the Glasgow train at Euston. They were at every stop waiting for him to get off, as they were reluctant to arrest him on the train knowing that he carried a gun. "When he left the train here in Carlisle, they arrested him and took him away. He'll be tried for murder. We thought you might have been involved when you began to make enquiries. I believe the American Police searched the trains believing that he had an accomplice, but found no one, but now we wonder if the G.I. who left your compartment was the other man we were looking for, and didn't return because he saw his friend arrested."

Liz had asked the question but was only half listening to his explanation, knowing that they had drawn the wrong conclusions about Joe. She was trying to work out why he had got off the train and not returned. And what of the diamonds? Had he known that they were fakes? Is that why he hadn't contacted her in Glasgow? Had he seen her with Howard? Had he been confident that she would take them to the fellow in Sauchiehall Street who would pretend that they were fakes so that Joe could have all the money? Was the Scottish soldier all part of the plan too?

It all seemed too risky for Joe to have relied on Liz doing exactly what he wanted her to, and what if things had gone wrong? He would then have lost the diamonds! No, it did not make sense to go to all that trouble. If Joe didn't want her to have some of the money, he need not have promised her any of it, or he could have just left her at home and never returned. As she got out of the car, she concluded that Joe must have been robbed by that soldier he had known, and that something had happened to him, but what she would probably never be able to discover.

She could not have envisaged at that time, that three months later she would learn that he had been murdered and his body dumped in the Clyde.

Liz sat quietly in the train as it sped towards London. She felt in her bag and took out the large diamond she had been told was worthless. She was still feeling hurt that she had lost all that money which she had hoped would make her rich. Suddenly she felt all alone. Howard would never want to see her again after the way she had deserted him. If only she had waited. He had not treated her in the way that Joe had done. When they had made love he had been more caring towards her. Suddenly, she began to miss him dreadfully, and longed to see him again. She could write and say that she was sorry about the way she had left him and send him the money for the hotel bill, but immediately had second thoughts about that. Perhaps he would not want to hear from her again after all that had happened.

She took one last look at the shiny stone in her hand then, in a sudden fit of temper, opened the window of the carriage, and threw it outside into the darkness.

CHAPTER EIGHT

In the next three months after returning to "The Cricketer's Arms", Liz tried to forget all about Joe, but now, after learning that he had been found murdered, she tried to work out what she should do. She had not been surprised that she had not heard from him after returning from Scotland as it had seemed obvious at the time that she had been used, and that there had been no intention of him giving her any of the money she had been promised. But now, perhaps those early conclusions had been wrong. If Joe had been killed soon after the time when she had thought he had been arrested, perhaps that Scottish soldier had been implicated. After all, it was he who had taken the real diamonds to Mr MacKenzie. The whole thing was a mystery.

The customers were surprised to see Liz so quiet that evening, and although she went to bed late as usual she couldn't sleep. She was convinced that the police would arrive early the next morning to question her, but first she had to contact Howard, and there was no time to write. She would have to go to Paisley immediately to try and see him.

She was now wide awake thinking about Howard. He had been in her thoughts constantly ever since she left Scotland, and she hoped that he had forgiven her for running away. She longed to see him again, but it was a long way to go just to say that she was sorry, and he might have even refused to see her. The one night they had spent together had been the happiest of her life, and had also been a turning point from the sort of life she had led previously. Now she had a perfectly good reason for going to see him, and felt excited at the prospect, in spite of the seriousness of the situation.

She was up very early, and met the postman as she had planned to do, then came back into the pub and put the letters on the table in the kitchen. She found some notepaper under the bar counter and went to her room to write a letter to herself. When her employer came into the kitchen, Liz appeared to be very upset and she was holding a letter in her hand.

"I had a letter from my Aunt in Glasgow this morning," she lied. "She's very ill and wondered whether I could possibly go and see her."

The landlord of the pub looked at her in disbelief. "You mean that you really do have an aunt in Glasgow, as well as the one here in the village?"

"Edith Harrison, here in the village, is my father's sister - she never married, and I really do have another aunt in Glasgow," she lied again. "She's my mother's widowed sister. I have written to her once since I came here, so that's how she knew where I was. She came down to London for the funeral when my mother and father were killed in that air-raid, and she told me then that I was her only relative...I really ought to go."

Cornelius Hill wasn't fully convinced that she was telling the truth. Liz had never mentioned her aunt in Glasgow before, except when she had used her as an excuse when she went to Scotland with Joe in January. He never thought that she ever existed, but now, she appeared to be really concerned about her sick aunt, but something didn't seem quite right to him.

"Can I see?" he asked, reaching out for the piece of paper she was holding. He thought that he recognised the type of paper she had used as he looked at the almost indecipherable scrawl written on it, but it looked genuine enough, with an address in Glasgow at the top, and dated three days previously. Liz had made a good job of it.

Cornelius turned the letter over, "No envelope?"

"Of course there was. I didn't bring it down. Can I go today, Neil?"

"If you must you must." Then he waved his hand in resignation, "Yes, of course you'd better go."

Cornelius searched for a while after Liz had left, and then found the writing pad she had used to write the fictitious letter. It confirmed his suspicion that there was no aunt in Glasgow, and Liz had gone to Scotland because of Joe's body turning up. He wondered how deeply she had been involved in the murder. Something had been worrying her ever since she had returned from Scotland, and a couple of times he had caught her in tears. Once he joked by telling her that he thought she was in love, and that had caused a real outburst. He had never questioned her as to why Joe had not come back, and assumed that he had rejoined his unit. When customers had asked her where her good looking American was, she had quickly changed the subject. He wondered who she was really going to see in Scotland, and decided that if anyone asked him where she was, he would tell them that she had gone to spend a few days in London.

Later that morning, two plain clothes policemen arrived at "The Cricketer's Arms," and asked Cornelius Hill if they could have a few words with Elizabeth Harrison.

Liz slept soundly on the train most of the way to Glasgow. However, at Carlisle, she awoke with a start as if an alarm had gone off in her head. She stared out of the carriage window. The early morning light gave the platform a strange peaceful look, and in complete contrast to when she and Howard had last looked out of the window at the dimly-lit station in January. She wondered whether Howard had thought any more about her since that time. As the train began to move again, she could see in her mind's eye the American being led away by the Military Police, whom they both thought at the time to have been Joe.

She suddenly realised that Howard would not have known that it had not been Joe taken away by the Military Police, unless he had recently seen the newspaper item reporting his murder. If he hadn't, then he could only have told the police, if they had already questioned him, that - as far as he knew - Joe had been arrested in Carlisle. However, if he had read the report of Joe's body being found in the Clyde, he would have been as surprised as she had been.

CHAPTER NINE

Howard was lying on his bed contemplating what had happened during the last twenty-four hours. He had already had two visits from the police. The first one had been the day before in response to the information they had received from the Carlisle police when they had interviewed Liz in January. He had been interrogated in the Padre's office about his knowledge of the American they had travelled with on the train, and was completely surprised when he learned that it wasn't Joe that they had seen arrested at Carlisle. The second visit he had had was again that morning. He was told that the local police in Dorset had visited the pub where Liz worked, but found that she wasn't there. The landlord had told the detectives that she was in London, but they knew that she had read about the American being murdered, and wondered whether she had contacted him here at H.M.S. Sanderling. They had asked Howard to let them know if she turned up.

For the last three months, Howard wasn't able to get what had happened out of his mind. It had not only been the disappointment about the diamonds or the loss of the money which constantly reminded him of those few days in January, but Liz herself who dominated his thoughts. Although they had spent so little time together, her departure had left a strange emptiness in his life. He had often thought about writing to her to arrange a meeting, but the manner of her leaving had prevented him from putting pen to paper, but now he just lay there thinking what might have happened since that day when Liz left him in that hotel. Had Joe been in contact with her he wondered, and why was he murdered and dumped in the Clyde? The police had told him that he had been in the water for months. Now, apparently, they couldn't find Liz. Where was she? It was all a mystery!

Meanwhile, Liz couldn't wait to see him. She hoped that he hadn't moved away. It crossed her mind that perhaps she ought to have written to him first, but she had been anxious to get away quickly in case the police came to the pub to question her. She realised that they could have been to see Howard already, and if he had managed to convince them that he knew nothing, then she had to know what to say when she was interviewed by them. If she had been questioned first, her story couldn't possibly have agreed with Howard's, as when the police had told her in Carlisle that it had not been Joe who had been arrested, he would not have known that. She hoped that he hadn't retaliated by telling the police about the faked diamonds, just because she had left him with a huge hotel bill to pay. She was not aware at this time that the one she had given him had been genuine. She knew that she had been right to come to see him. If only the train would hurry!

By the time she had grabbed a sandwich and a cup of tea on Glasgow's Central Station, and caught a tram to Paisley, then walked the mile or so to the gates of the Royal Naval Air Station at Abbotsinch, it was late morning. She asked the white-gaitered guard if it was possible to see Air Mechanic Howard Hartwell, as it was very urgent, but she didn't know his number.

"Urgent is it?" the guard asked in his broad South Wales accent. "You'll be his second visitor this morning now. He's already had two plain clothes policemen to see him. He must be very important but no criminal, as they didn't take him away see. Who shall I say wants to see him, and what for? There is a war on, you know. You might be a spy - mind you, a very pretty one."

Liz felt the blood rushing to her cheeks. It took a lot to make her blush, but very few girls apart from the W.R.N.S came to the

72

gatehouse, and this handsome Welshman was enjoying flirting with her. It was obviously true what they said about sailors, she decided. His manner reminded her of Howard. Her reason for wanting to see him had to sound convincing.

"I've come for the same reason as the police, and all the way from Dorset. Please, it's very important that I see him."

"Well, the police have only just left. It's a wonder that you didn't see their car. It's nearly time for the mid-day meal, so we should catch him before he goes back to the hangars on the other side of the airfield."

He flicked a switch and spoke into a microphone. Loudspeakers throughout the camp boomed out the message. "D'yer hear there. D'yer hear there. Would Air Mechanic Howard Hartwell report to the main gate immediately. This message is urgent."

When the announcement came over the tannoy that he was to report to the gatehouse, it wasn't as much of a shock as it might have been if the police hadn't already spoken to him about their assumption that Liz might come to see him. He suspected that the call for him to report at the gatehouse was because she was there. He wasn't surprised to see her. They stood looking at each other for a few seconds neither knowing what to say, then, Liz moved forward and gave him a kiss in greeting. Howard smiled and gave her a hug in return. He thought she looked older, and her face was a peculiar shade of pinkish grey. They moved away from the watching guard before he spoke. There was no need for him to ask why she was here, or for her to explain.

"So it wasn't Joe who was arrested," he began.

Liz looked surprised. "How did you find out? "Have the police been to see you? What have you told them?" She now wanted to know the answers quickly.

"They've been to see me twice, and they told me the second time that they hadn't been able to find you," he said, and without waiting for her reaction, asked, "When did you see Joe last. Do you know who murdered him?"

Liz looked shocked that Howard should suspect that she knew who might have killed Joe, and explained what had happened at Carlisle police station in January where she had found out that it had not been Joe who had been arrested. She said that she was sorry that she had not told him before.

Howard told her about his interrogations and that he had told them nothing which would lead the police to suspect that they had been involved in any way with Joe's death.

"I didn't tell them anything about the diamonds, but they didn't ask me anyway. By the way, Liz, how much did you get for your diamond?"

"What diamond?"

"The one that you took out of the packet at the hotel before we took them to that lying jeweller. You do now realise that they were ALL real, and we were swindled."

Liz's eyes opened wide in disbelief, "What do you mean, 'real'? I threw mine away after that jeweller had told us that the others were fakes."

"Fakes? I got eight-hundred-and-fifty pounds for mine, and even then I was robbed!"

"Tell me more," Liz asked.

Howard explained what happened after she left him in the hotel, and how he had managed to use the money from the diamond he had sold to pay the hotel bill. He didn't know who had been involved in swindling them, but, he thought, it must have included both the Scottish soldier, and the jeweller, and perhaps even Joe.

"I have thought about it many times," he told her, "but can't work out what really happened. What I am certain of, is that they were too good for us - whoever "they" were."

"I'm sorry I left you to pay the hotel bill, Howard, but I've brought enough money with me to pay back what it cost you." Her face had returned to its natural colour, and her eyes looked a lot

74

more kindly than before.

"There's no need for that, Liz. Remember I told you how much I got for the diamond from a jeweller in the hotel, and that..." Howard stopped in mid sentence. "Oh my god! I've just realised that if they find out where we stayed in Glasgow, the Hotel Manager will remember me - he arranged the sale. There can't be many people in navy uniform who have to pay their hotel bill with a diamond! Once they've identified me from my name in the register, it's only one more question away from knowing that we both stayed there, and then the details of who booked the hotel will be revealed, and...oh god! it's a real hornet's nest. Look Liz, they know here that the police have been to question me, so it should be fairly easy for me to get a couple of days compassionate leave to try and sort things out. I'll meet you as soon as possible in that cafe in the high street." He took hold of her hand as he spoke and she made no attempt to stop him. The guard watched her go, never taking his eyes off her shapely legs until she disappeared round a bend in the road.

Liz waited impatiently until Howard arrived at the cafe. It seemed a lifetime since he had passed the diamonds to her over the table. She had chosen to sit in the same seats that they had sat in three months earlier, and the same red-headed girl who had served them the last time took their order. Howard looked across the table into those beautiful green eyes and recalled the conversation they had had there previously. He remembered how she had teased him by offering him a bonus if he went with her back to the hotel. That had excited him, and he was aware of that same feeling now. Grinning broadly, he asked facetiously, "Are you going to offer me the same as you did the last time we were here?" She didn't respond with a smile as he expected, but had a look in her eyes he hadn't seen before.

"I hope," she began in almost a whisper, "no, I mean, I wish...." She looked at Howard, unable to continue, suddenly realising how much she loved this man sitting opposite her. It was a sort of love that she hadn't experienced before, but now he was teasing her about what had happened the last time they were here, and she felt ashamed about the way she had acted then.

Howard noticed that her hands were shaking a little as they rested on the table. He took them gently into his. They felt soft, almost without life. It wasn't hard to see what Liz was trying to say, and the look in her eyes told him what he wanted to know. She had never really been out of his thoughts. Leaning forward, he said quietly, "Liz, I've missed you so, and I think I'm in love with you."

She wanted to tell him that she loved him too, but if she spoke now she knew that she would burst into tears like a schoolgirl. A tear trickled down her cheek and Howard knew that there was no need for her to say anything. He handed her his handkerchief and told her to dry her eyes.

"Why are we being so unhappy?" Howard said, giving her a smile.

She smiled back, and, now able to speak, told him that she too was in love with him, and how much she had missed him. "I feel better now that you're here. I didn't know what to do when I saw Joe's photograph in the newspaper."

He bent down and kissed her hands. "We'll do nothing for the moment. I just want to sit here with you and forget all what has happened before."

"But we can't. We will have to go to the police sometime and explain what we know. They probably suspect us as being involved with Joe's murder. What are we to do, Howard?"

Howard felt that he had to take hold of the situation as Liz appeared to be unable to think clearly. "Well, my sweet, the first thing we have to do is find somewhere for you to stay. Did you bring a case?"

Liz shook her head. "I never thought of that," she said,

grinning, "I wanted to see you so desperately that it never entered my mind to even bring a case or any change of clothes - and I never thought of a nightie!"

"That's the last thing you'll need tonight," Howard chuckled.

They left the cafe, and noticed for the first time that the sun was shining and that it was a glorious spring day. They found a small hotel in Moss Street, and with her appetite returned, Liz suddenly announced that apart from a few sandwiches, she had had very little to eat since she left the village the day before. Howard hadn't eaten any breakfast either, so they sat in the restaurant of the small hotel they had found, and enjoyed a meal together.

"We have very little to worry about, really," Howard said, trying to reassure her. "We haven't murdered anybody, stolen anything, or committed any crime as far as I can see."

"But what about the diamonds?" Liz asked, still sounding worried in spite of Howard's confidence that everything would be alright. "There are many at that hotel in Glasgow who will remember us."

"I've had second thoughts about that. There's only the diamond that I sold in the hotel to worry about, and I'll have to think of something to explain that. There's no reason at all, as far as I can see, that the police will be able to find out about the diamonds, or that they even existed. Think about it, Liz. The only people who knew we had them were Joe, who is dead, the jeweller, and that Scottish soldier who supposedly brought the real ones to him earlier. The last two are bound to keep quiet."

Howard had often thought about that soldier, and what part he had played to do them out of the money. The man had booked the room, presumably at Joe's request, and also brought a bottle of champagne to the hotel. He either must have been well paid or had planned to get the diamonds for himself. Howard knew that it would be hard to explain why they had drunk the bottle of champagne if the police found out about it, especially as it had been brought there by someone they didn't know, but then he suddenly had an idea about what had happened.

"I think that I've just solved it, Liz," Howard said slowly and deliberately. "What if that soldier arranged to meet Joe at Carlisle - that's why Joe insisted on getting off the train - then prevented him from getting back on, murdered him, and arranged with the jeweller to lie to us to enable him to get the money. He would have to wait until we had taken the diamonds to him, of course, which we did."

"And that's where your theory goes wrong, my darling amateur detective," Liz said a friendly mocking way. "Do you think that he would take that risk after doing a murder? What if we hadn't taken them to the jeweller, and what guarantee did he have that we knew where to take them? And come to think of it, how did the body come to be in the Clyde near Glasgow?"

"You're right, clever girl. As a detective, I make a good mechanic. However, I'm still a little worried about the diamond, and that bottle of champagne."

"Well we've finished our lunch, and I think that we can worry about those things later", Liz said. "Meanwhile let's go and look at our room." Howard didn't miss the wink she gave him.

Detective Inspector Alistair McIntosh felt annoyed at what he had thought was going to be an army problem, was now beginning to look like being a long drawn out murder case for him to solve. He was convinced that it would certainly delay his retirement.

After interviewing the missing girl's boy friend at the Naval Air Station, he had dismissed the theory that the murdered American soldier had had anything to do with the one who had been arrested at Carlisle in January, but thought that the girl must know more about this G.I. than she had told them at the time, and that probably went for the sailor as well. But why had the murdered victim got off the train at Carlisle when he had told them that he was going to Glasgow, and what had happened to him after that? Why should anyone strangle him and put his body into the Clyde? Perhaps all this would become clear when he was able to question that girl and her sailor boyfriend together.

The inspector called his sergeant into his office. "Have you done all those enquiries I asked you to do, Baillie?"

"I have, sir - just finished them. I did the last phone call about two minutes ago."

"Well, don't mess about, man, what have you found out?"

"The girl stayed at the Renfield Hotel in St.Enoch's Square for four nights, and was joined by Hartwell on Tuesday. The hotel understood that they were married. Then she left, and he stayed on for another night. What I don't understand, sir, is that he sold a diamond to pay the bill."

"Did you say a diamond, Sergeant? What sort of a diamond? Do you mean a diamond ring?"

"The manager said it was just a diamond. He didn't mention a ring."

"People don't just carry diamonds around with them, Sergeant, least of all Fleet Air Arm Air Mechanics! You'd better check on that. What else?"

"Well, they booked in the hotel as Mr. and Mrs. Hartwell, but the room had already been booked in advance of their arrival by a Scottish soldier named..." The sergeant opened his notebook and flipped over a couple of pages, "....named McKern. He booked the room in the name of Mr and Mrs Harrison, and here's the queer part. He left a bottle of champagne for the couple to celebrate their honeymoon with."

"I don't believe for one moment that Hartwell and the girl were husband and wife, Sergeant. Hartwell said nothing about being married when we interviewed him, and her name is still Harrison. I think they met on the train, had an affair in the hotel as he told us, and then she went back suddenly, leaving him to pay the bill, meanwhile, the American may have turned up and was murdered. So where is this Mr. Harrison who she was supposed to be married to? - who is this soldier who miraculously produced a bottle of Bollinger and booked the hotel in the first place? - and where did Hartwell get that diamond? Three questions, maybe four, need answering, Baillie, or are we on some wild goose chase? Perhaps none of them had anything to do with this murdered American?. Has anyone found the girl yet?"

"Well yes, I think so."

"What do you mean, 'you think so'? Have you or haven't you?"

"She's been seen by the Naval guards at the camp, and met our sailor friend..." Inspector Alistair McIntosh interrupted his sergeant, "Don't call him our friend, Baillie, he could be our murderer, but go on."

"Well, nothing else really. She met him and they had a long talk at the camp gates, and then she went off."

"Do you mean you've lost her, Baillie?"

"I'm afraid we have sir, but the guard heard them say that they arranged to meet, and Hartwell left the camp an hour or so later. I could go back and question him again sir when he goes back on board."

Inspector McIntosh looked at his sergeant in disbelief. "On board! Baillie?" Since when have you been using nautical terms. It's an airfield!"

"I think in the Fleet Air Arm, they call it a concrete aircraft-carrier, sir. 'Back on board' is a phrase they use when...."

Alistair interrupted him. "I know all that, Sergeant, let's get on with it, shall we?"

"There's nothing left to tell, sir. We'll have to wait until he goes back and hopefully she turns up as well."

The inspector held his head in despair. "What a way to run an enquiry!" and then added sarcastically, "I suppose you're waiting for that mysterious Scotsman who booked them into the hotel to turn up as well are you, Sergeant? What's his name? McKern isn't it? Have you tried the War Office, Baillie?"

"There must be hundreds of McKerns, sir."

"Well, you've got to start somewhere. It's no good sitting around here...." Alistair stopped what he was going to say as he suddenly thought of something. "Tell you what, Sergeant, try the jewellers' shops in Glasgow first: there are fewer of them. If diamonds are part of this jigsaw, then a jeweller may know something. Try the back street ones first," and then added as an afterthought, "And go and find out whether the hotel had seen an American G.I. at the same time that Hartwell and the girl stayed there."

Alistair considered that he wasn't making much progress, but perhaps his sergeant would discover some clues in the enquiries he was to make among the jewellers. He still believed that the key to this murder was the girl. He swore quietly at his sergeant's incompetence of not organising a twenty-four hour watch on the Naval Station which allowed the girl to slip through their fingers, and further delay the investigation. His retirement seemed much further away now than it did a week ago.

CHAPTER TEN

On the journey to Glasgow in January, Joe had got off the train at Carlisle as he had previously arranged to do, joining in with the other passengers on the platform so as not to be too conspicuous. He had gone straight to the waiting room to meet Andy, whom he found sitting in a dimly-lit corner looking worried.

"Have you seen the Military Police?" were his first words to Joe, "There's a few of them aboot the station."

"I didn't see any of 'em on the platform, but there were a couple of sons-of-bitches at Euston I had to avoid." Joe sounded concerned. "Maybe I'll have to be careful when I get back on the train. Are all the arrangements the same as yer told me in December?" he asked.

It was the main reason why Joe had wanted to see the man who had fixed everything for him in Glasgow, as he didn't want anything to go wrong at the last minute. Andy assured him that the arrangements he had made still stood. Joe waited a few more minutes, looking out continually to see if the platform was clear before returning to the train, when suddenly there was a commotion. He saw two M.Ps running across the platform towards the front of the train. There was a lot of shouting and the few people left on the platform were standing still, watching whatever was happening towards the front of the train. "What's going on?" Andy asked him.

"I don't know, but maybe yer ought to go and have a look before I make a dash to get back."

Andy went outside but returned after a little while. "The place is full of Military Police, and it looks as if two of them have just arrested an American soldier who put up something of a struggle. You'll be seen if you go now - unless you want t'risk it."

Joe hesitated too long before making a decision. He heard a whistle blow and realised that the train was about to leave. If he ran out now, he thought, he would be noticed, and certainly recognised by his uniform as an American soldier. Possibly they would think that he was an accomplice of the one who had been arrested. He decided that he wouldn't risk it.

"Oh, what the hell! I'll come and stay with you, Andy, if I can, and catch a train later in the mornin'. Liz'll soon realize I've missed the dern train, and wait for me when she gets to the hotel. She knows where we are going to stay." Joe was convinced that he had nothing to worry about.

He arrived in Glasgow later that afternoon and went straight to the hotel, saw the porter, gave his name as Harrison, and asked which room his wife was in.

"What was the name again, sir?"

"Harrison."

The porter looked through the book. "I'm sorry sir, but we don't have a Mrs. Harrison staying here. The name has been deleted and a Mr.and Mrs.Hartwell have taken the room. Had you cancelled, it sir?"

Joe was completely taken aback by this. "When was this done?" he asked, anxiously. "Do yer know who cancelled it?" Joe gave him a full description of Liz.

"I'm afraid I don't know, sir, and I haven't seen the person you described. This must have happened before I came on duty."

Joe sat down on one of the easy chairs and ordered a coffee. A Mr.and Mrs. Hartwell he had said. This couldn't be Liz, so where could she be? If she had cancelled the room reservation, why had she done it? He could ask the porter who had been on duty at the time, but he would have to wait until later that evening or the next morning. Meanwhile he would book a room and wait to see if she turned up. He could also check with the jeweller in case she tried to sell the diamonds without him, but she would know that he would arrive sometime, so it would be ludicrous for her to do so. In any case, the appointment had been made for next Wednesday, and today was only Saturday!

Joe suddenly realized that he had nothing but the clothes he stood up in. He had left his suitcase containing the rest of his things with the diamonds on the train, and he needed to get them back from Liz, but where was she? After making the various enquiries, he left the hotel to go and buy some personal items, and anything else he thought he would require for the one night. Surely Liz would turn up soon, he thought, dismissing any previous conjectures about her non-appearance. Joe began to feel more certain that it had been Liz who had cancelled their booking and, when he returned to the hotel, he thought that it would be a good idea to check with the Hartwells to see if they had seen Liz, and whether she had given them any reason for cancelling their reservation.

"I've checked the room, sir, but there doesn't appear to be either of the Hartwells in at the moment." The porter sounded almost apologetic, although he looked at Joe somewhat suspiciously.

Sometime later as Joe sat reading a newspaper in the foyer, he was astounded to hear the voice of Elizabeth asking for her room key. She was alone and she made no enquiry about whether he himself had arrived. He hid behind his paper until she had gone to the lift, then went over to the desk.

"Mrs Hartwell has just arrived, sir," the porter informed him.

"Oh yeah? You must be kiddin'!" Joe could hardly believe what he had said. "Have yer seen *Mr*. Hartwell?" he asked innocently.

"I understand that he is in the Royal Navy, sir, and will be joining her later," the porter told him.

Joe thought deeply about the situation as he walked back to where he'd been sitting. So that was it. It must be that sailor they had met on the train. It couldn't have been anyone else. How did they think they would get away with whatever they were plotting? Surely they knew that he would turn up. If they were planning to steal the diamonds that he had left on the train, why hadn't she gone to another hotel? What made her so certain that he wouldn't be here? He then remembered the incident on Carlisle station and the arrest of the American soldier. Maybe they saw the G.I. being taken away by the Military Police and assumed it to have been him. He concluded that that must be the only explanation possible.

Now it all fitted together. Joe suddenly recalled the sailor's name as being Howard. He walked back to the desk. "Can I have another look at the reservations book? Do'yer mind?"

The porter turned it round so that he could read the names. 'Mr.and Mrs. H.Hartwell.' Joe felt angry. It was obvious that they were going to keep the appointment with the jeweller and keep the money for themselves. "That son-of-a-bitch sailor had soon stepped into my shoes," he said to himself, "and only hours after he thought that he had seen me arrested!" He decided that he would keep out of sight and see what developed. He booked a room in the hotel under a fictitious name and by the next morning he had worked out a plan. He saw Liz go out on Sunday morning, and was about to follow her, when Andy walked into the hotel.

"What are yer doin' here?" Joe asked, "I didn't expect to see you until after I'd taken the diamonds to that jeweller fella on Wednesday evening, but I'm mighty glad yer came."

Joe explained to him what he thought Liz and the sailor were up to, and that he had worked out a plan to exclude Liz from her share of the diamonds. "It'll serve her right, but for the moment I'm keepin' it to myself. I'm goin' to visit your Charlie MacKenzie tomorro' mornin' and explain to him what I want him to do."

"I dinna mind what you do as long as my money is safe," Andy said, laughing, and wished Joe luck.

CHAPTER ELEVEN

Sergeant Baillie entered Charlie MacKenzie's jeweller's shop late in the morning. He had already visited about half the shops on his list and had the rest to do in the afternoon. He introduced himself and took out Joe's photograph which the police had obtained from the "Daily Mirror."

"You've no doubt seen the report in all the papers of a murdered American soldier..."

Charlie shook his head. He never bought newspapers. He considered them a waste of money when the wireless could give him all the news that he wanted to know. The sergeant noticed the jeweller's negative response but carried on to ask the question that he had put to all the others as he showed him the photograph. "Have you seen this American soldier before, and has he ever visited your shop?"

Charlie went pale as he looked at the photograph. In a moment, he relived the events of three months earlier. Charlie shook his head again, "No, no, I've never seen him before," he lied unconvincingly. Charlie wasn't very good at lying. Sergeant Baillie didn't believe him. He could see the drops of perspiration on the shopkeeper's forehead and upper lip.

"This man's body was found in the Clyde at Bothwell. He'd been in the water some time, Mr. MacKenzie. We want to find out who killed him." He looked closely at the slightly bent, white-haired man. "It would help if you could remember if he came into your shop to buy or sell you something. Can you recall when he came here?"

Sergeant Baillie was an experienced policeman. He knew his job, and he knew that this was the time to keep quiet. He had asked an important question and waited for an answer.

At first, Charlie thought that the policeman had known that Joe had been there, but as he hadn't told him that the American had been strangled, he assumed that the sergeant didn't know. Perhaps they thought that he had drowned. The only problem was that he had to tell another lie.

"Let me have another look at that photograph." Charlie held out his hand to take the photograph off the sergeant. He felt calmer now. "No, I don't remember him. Why? what's he done to get murdered?"

"That's what we're trying to find out. Are you absolutely sure that you don't recognise this man and that he hasn't been here to sell you some diamonds."

The word 'diamonds' took him by surprise. Charlie's hand began to shake a little which he steadied by placing it on the counter. "I'm absolutely sure, officer. Were they stolen?"

"I'll ask the questions if you don't mind, sir." Sergeant Baillie considered leaving at that point and bringing in the inspector, but then re-considered the situation, feeling capable enough of handling it himself. "Why did you ask if they were stolen?"

Charlie realised that he shouldn't have asked that. He knew, of course, that the diamonds had been stolen and that must have been at the forefront of his mind when he had asked. He wondered whether the sergeant knew more than he was prepared to tell him. "I just thought that's why he'd been murdered." Charlie was beginning to panic now, and he wished he hadn't started it. Thankfully, the sergeant appeared to dismiss Charlie's comments, putting his obvious nervousness down to his age.

The sergeant had only asked him about diamonds to carry out his inspector's theory. "One final question, sir. Do you know anyone by the name of McKern, a soldier?"

Charlie felt his mouth go dry. He had to lie yet again. He wasn't going to admit that he had known Andy for as many years as he cared to remember, but he knew that the police would not be able to make enquiries on those lines because the shop where Andy had worked before the war was now closed and the owner had died. "No, Sergeant, I've never known anyone with that name." Charlie was surprised how convincing his own voice had sounded.

"If we need to ask you any more questions we'll be back." Sergeant Baillie closed his notebook and put away the photograph.

When the policeman had gone, Charlie went to the back of the shop and poured himself a generous tot of Johnny Walker's which he kept for special occasions, and he considered that this had been one of them. He would like to have told the policeman all that he knew but didn't know how to do it without involving himself. He poured himself another double Scotch.

Later that afternoon, Liz and Howard waited until the shop was empty before entering. Charlie looked up and the blood drained from his face. It was the second shock that he'd had that day. He could tell by the expression on their faces that they had not come to congratulate him or renew acquaintances. Howard pulled down the blind on the door and suggested that Charlie should lock it. Charlie made no objection, but collected his keys from the back of the shop and did as he was told. He feared that he would be forced to tell what had taken place three months earlier.

"Now, Charlie, we would like to know the truth. As you probably know, Joe's been found dead." Charlie nodded his head, and Howard continued without pausing, "and we believe that you know what happened. When you lied to us about the diamonds, we'd like to know why, and what you hoped to gain."

Charlie put up both his hands to stop his interrogator. "I've already had the police here this morning and told them nothing, but I have to tell someone what I know, otherwise I'll go mad. It'll perhaps ensure that I'll have a good night's rest for the first time since January. You'd better come to the back of the shop and sit down. It's a long story..."

A week ago, Detective Inspector Alistair McIntosh had been looking forward to retirement, but now his old ulcer was beginning to play him up. He stirred a spoonful of bicarbonate of soda into some milk which he drank before looking up at his sergeant.

"Right, Baillie, this is what we have so far. We have a deserter from the American Army who takes his girl to Glasgow pretending to be on honeymoon. A soldier with the name of McKern takes a bottle of champagne and books a room in a hotel a week or two before they arrive. She then makes out that a sailor, Howard Hartwell, who was travelling with them, was her boyfriend, and they both think they see the American G.I., Joe Peabody..." the inspector shook his head, "What a name, Peabody!...being arrested on Carlisle Station, but it turned out not to have been him after all. The porter at the hotel has now told us that an American G.I. enquired about the room later on the same day that that girl Elizabeth Harrison arrived. The room had been booked in her name by McKern which she then changed to Hartwell. I'm certain that that American must be our murder victim. By using Hartwell's name, the girl - who, I might remind you, Sergeant, you still have not found - appears to have planned from the outset to have an affair with the sailor as soon as she reached the hotel, which, apparently, only lasted for one night and two days! Now why did she do that, Baillie? And why didn't the American make his presence known to her? She told the Carlisle police that she hadn't seen him since he had got off the train!"

"Perhaps the American had wanted her to believe that he had

been taken away by the army, sir, to watch what she was up to."

"Highly unlikely, Sergeant. How could he have known that she mistook that other soldier who was arrested by the Military Police for him? Then, on her return to London after doing a bunk, she deliberately got off the train at Carlisle to make enquiries about the American, and left Hartwell to pay the hotel bill. This he did by selling a diamond to a jeweller introduced to him by the hotel manager."

Baillie looked puzzled. "I wonder why he did that, sir. Should we not find out where he got that diamond from? I can't question him until he returns to the aircraft...." the sergeant nearly added the word 'carrier', but remembered how his inspector had reacted last time he used the Fleet Air Arm name for the Naval Air Station, and quickly changed it to..."the airfield."

Alistair looked at his sergeant in disbelief."Why can't you question him? Where is he? You haven't lost HIM now?"

"He's taken a few days leave, and no one knows where he's gone, except that I think he's gone off with that girl we believe to be Elizabeth Harrison."

"I don't believe it!" The inspector put his head in his hands. "What about the jewellers, Baillie? Any success there?"

"No, sir. No one saw or knew either the American or McKern, or had dealt with diamonds in January. There was one old man who I thought knew more than he told me at first, but he wouldn't murder anybody or have been involved in a murder. He was a nice old boy, really, but I frightened him. I think."

"You're not supposed to think, Sergeant, you're supposed to act, and your next move is to find that soldier McKern."

CHAPTER TWELVE

Back in January, Howard and Liz left Charlie MacKenzie's shop thoroughly disappointed that they had come away without the thousands of pounds they had expected to receive, and completely at a loss to understand how they had come to have faked diamonds in their possession. As soon as they had left the premises, Andy McKern came out of his hiding place at the back of the shop.

"You did that well, Charlie, and you followed Joe's instructions to the letter. Thank God they believed what you said."

Charlie had done everything that Joe had told him when he had visited him two days earlier, but now he felt a little sorry for the girl by sending her away with a measly few pounds, when the diamonds she had brought had been really worth a couple of hundred-thousand.

Today was Andy's second visit to Charlie within a few days. He had been there on Monday when Joe had visited Charlie to tell him what he wanted him to do when he expected Liz and Howard to bring him the diamonds, but for reasons that Charlie did not understand, Andy had remained hidden from Joe all the time. Andy heard Joe tell Charlie that he was certain that Liz thought that he had been arrested, and for him to tell her when she came, that firstly, the diamonds were fakes and worthless, and secondly, that the real stones had already been given to him by the Scottish soldier who had booked her hotel reservation. Joe had gone on to explain to Charlie that the girl was obviously planning to share the money for the diamonds with her new boyfriend. So if Charlie would tell them that the diamonds were fakes then that would get rid of the sailor, and give Liz her just rewards - which was nothing!

Charlie had felt quite intimidated at the time, knowing that if he didn't go along with Joe's plan, he would probably get nothing himself, but he couldn't help wondering why Andy had kept his presence unknown to Joe as he remained hidden, listening to their conversation. He was also surprised that Andy was only asking £10,000 for his part in all this, when he must have known that the diamonds were worth a considerable amount more. He was also worried about what was going on, but when Andy had told him that he would be back on Wednesday to see Joe, he considered that his suspicions were unfounded.

In spite of this, after Andy had left, Charlie began to feel a little afraid of him. When he had known Andy before the war as a young apprentice in the trade, he had had a reputation for being a little ruthless, but now, no doubt due to his training as a commando, he appeared hard and his manner threatening. Nor did he care much for his friend who had driven him to Glasgow in an army van. Andy had explained that as he was now unable to drive because of his arm, his fellow commando had managed to borrow the vehicle which had brought them there.

On that cold Wednesday night in January, Joe had followed closely behind Liz and Howard as they walked from the hotel to the jewellers. He had felt particularly bitter and angry as he had seen them arm in arm in the hotel going to their room the previous evening, and again later, when he saw them in the restaurant drinking the champagne that Andy had taken to the hotel - originally meant for himself and Liz. When he was aware that they had spent the night together, he felt like murdering her, and was glad that he'd had the foresight to ensure that she would have nothing. He even began to hate her as he watched her from a discreet distance, striding out to the jeweller's where she was hoping to receive the £50,000. He smiled to himself, thinking how he would have liked to have seen their faces when Charlie MacKenzie told them that the stones were worthless.

Joe did not have to wait very long after they had entered the premises of the jeweller in the little side street, before they came out again. Liz, striding out much quicker than when she had arrived there, and obviously angry, with Howard following behind and trying to catch her up. Joe chuckled quietly to himself as he hid in the shadows. It had worked. Now he was ready to collect his £50,000. What he did not know, was that Andy was already there, and had watched the proceedings from his hiding place in the shop.

By the time Joe knocked on the door, Andy had already collected his own cut of £10,000, and had gone into the other room to join his friend who had brought him to Glasgow in the army vehicle. Charlie MacKenzie opened the door of his premises, greeting Joe with a huge smile.

"I've got them, Joe, and on the whole they are a magnificent lot. I'm extremely pleased, but I couldn't help feeling sorry for the girl. You didn't tell me how pretty she was."

"She didn't look very pretty after she left here," Joe quipped, "In fact she looked positively angry." While Joe was talking, he watched Charlie close the outside door, and then open the safe to take out the money he had been promised. Charlie realized that Joe would not have seen the letter he had sent to the hotel reducing his offer, and thought it now best to say nothing. "Here you are Joe, £50,000, and don't spend it all at once."

"When are yer expectin' Andy to come for his cut?" Joe asked out of curiosity.

"I'm here now Joe." Andy emerged from the other room, and went to where the two men were standing. The atmosphere in the room didn't seem quite right, and Joe noticed that there was

93

something unusual about Andy's tone of voice. This should have been a joyous occasion, but Andy looked very sinister. The other soldier followed Andy out and stood next to Joe causing him to feel uncomfortable.

"Who's this son-of-a...?"

Andy interrupted Joe before he finished the question by remarking somewhat sarcastically, "I understand that you were arrested on Carlisle station, Joe."

Joe forced a slight chuckle. "Don't talk silly, man. What's all this about?"

"But your girl friend thinks you've been arrested," Andy said in that same mocking voice.

Joe looked hard at Andy and tried to keep calm. "But I dern well told you that in the hotel". He was beginning to suspect what the Scotsman was up to, and he became tense in anticipation of what might happen. He was annoyed with himself for leaving it this late to come and collect his money. He should have waited until the morning.

"And, if you're in prison," Andy continued, "you winna need all that money." He pointed in the direction of the pile of white notes.

Joe perceived a slight nod of Andy's head, but before he could react, the other soldier had his hands around Joe's neck applying enormous pressure. For a second or two, Joe made an involuntary sickening sound deep in the back of his throat, his eyes and mouth opening wide. Charlie let out a stifled cry of protest as, spellbound, he watched Joe's body fall down heavily on to the floor, and then lie still in a crumpled heap.

Charlie's blood drained from his face and his body began to shake. He had had no inkling of what Andy had planned to do. He felt fear as he had never experienced it before. He now realised that he was in the presence of two ruthless trained killers, and began to fear for his own life. "Is he dead?" he asked, half under his breath.

"He's dead alright," Andy's friend remarked coolly, not even bending down to check. He had done this type of thing before, but previously the victims had always been German soldiers.

"Right, Charlie," Andy said, calmly picking up the money that had been for Joe, "We'll get rid o' the body, and then we'll be off. Oh, and by the way, I widna tell anyone about this if I were you, or somebody may find out aboot those diamonds in your safe! Alright?"

Charlie was still shaking uncontrollably as he stood speechless. The other soldier had left the building, and had brought the vehicle to just outside the door, then he told Andy that it was safe to bring out the body.

"Dinna worry about this chap, Charlie," Andy remarked. "Naebody will miss him - only his mither - if she's still alive." He laughed, and went out of the door dragging Joe's corpse.

After Charlie MacKenzie had explained to Elizabeth and Howard what took place that night when they had left the shop, they wondered how this quiet little man could have been party to everything that had happened. Firstly, the deceit he had perpetrated on behalf of those criminals, and, secondly, the way that he had been able to convince them when they had brought the real diamonds to him, that they were fakes and worthless. However, Liz suddenly began to feel sorry for this pathetic old man. Joe's brutal murder had placed him in an unenviable position. He would not be able to tell the police about how Joe had been murdered for fear of what might happen to him if he did, especially after keeping quiet about it all this time.

"But you haven't done badly out if it," Howard said. "I suppose that you still have the diamonds or have benefited from their value by selling them."

Charlie shook his head."I've never made any money from the diamonds. They are all in a safe deposit box in my bank, and the money I paid out has left me with a huge overdraft. I can't even bear to look at the stones, let alone sell them to the trade. So what good has it done me? I see Joe's murder in my dreams every night - that is when I'm able to get any sleep at all."

Liz and Howard had gone to the shop feeling sorry for themselves at being swindled out of a fortune, but they didn't envy the old man's plight. Indeed, Howard began to wonder how they could help him.

"Where are these two fellows, Andy McKern and his mate?" Howard asked. "Do you know?"

"I expect they could be traced quite easily if they haven't left the army or deserted. Andy told me that he was going to have some hospital treatment for his arm. I believe the surgeons are going to try and repair it for him."

"What was wrong with his arm?" Liz asked.

"He'd been shot in the shoulder and his nerves were damaged. It could be that he's had an operation already."

Liz looked at Howard, "If it was that bad, he would have needed a few operations. We could go round to the hospitals and make enquiries."

Charlie looked worried. "Now, hold on a minute, you two. If the police find him he's bound to try and save his own skin by telling them that his mate killed Joe. Then the police will find out about the diamonds and I'll be in serious trouble. I can't risk it. Leave it alone and go back home. I'll give you five-hundred pounds each if you forget it. Tell the police nothing. Don't worry about me. I feel better already now that I've told somebody."

"We'll think about it and come and see you again before we go."

Liz clung on to Howard's arm as they left the shop. "What are we going to do, Howard? We can't leave it like this, but I like the idea of the money he's offered."

The next day, Howard was due back at the Station, and Liz walked with him down the narrow road alongside the river Cart in the early morning sunshine. What they did not expect to see was a uniformed policeman coming out of the gatehouse as they approached the Naval Air station.

"Mr Hartwell?" the policeman looked very serious. Howard nodded. "And you'll be Miss Harrison. Am I right, miss?"

"You're quite right, officer. I suppose you want to talk to me as well."

"Not me, miss. I've already been in touch with the CID in Glasgow when I saw you the two of you coming down the road, and they're sending a car. Perhaps you'll both wait here until they come if you wouldn't mind."

"We'd be delighted," Howard quipped, and grinned at Liz. "Remember what we've agreed," he whispered.

When the car eventually arrived, Sergeant Baillie was in the front seat. He got out and approached the couple.

"I would like you to come with me to the police station, if you don't mind. Detective Inspector McIntosh would like to ask you some questions about that American G.I. that was found dead."

Howard grinned again at Liz. "Everyone's being very polite about it," he said to her, and then, turning to the sergeant, he teased, "What if we refused."

"Ah, then I would have to arrest you on suspicion of being involved in the murder of Private Joseph Peabody, sir, and you wouldn't want that would you sir, especially the young lady?" The sergeant looked at Liz and gave her a kindly smile.

"You must be joking," Howard said in a voice that sounded as though he was dismissing the suggestion.

"I'd like you to save what you have to say until we get to the station, I think that it would be best, sir."

Howard shrugged his shoulders, resigning himself to the inevitable as they both got into the back seat of the car.

CHAPTER THIRTEEN

Andy McKern was in the Glasgow Royal Infirmary, recovering from the second operation on his shoulder to try and repair the damage that has been done by that German sniper's bullet. He would probably have to lose his arm, but the doctors hadn't yet given up hope that they might be able to save it.

He opened his locker and took out the "Daily Mirror", which had been in there for a few days. He hadn't felt like reading it at the time because of the pain he was suffering, but was now feeling much better. After glancing at the headlines, he turned to the centre pages. Joe's face stared at him just below the story of how the body had been discovered in the Clyde. His heart missed a beat, and then as he read that the police were appealing for witnesses, he relaxed a little when he realised that the only two were his friend, Sid, who had helped him dispose of the body after killing him, and Charlie MacKenzie, the jeweller had watched the murder take place. The story in the paper told how Joe had been identified from his tag which was still round his neck when the police found him. He could not understand how both he and Sid had forgotten to remove it, but could not even remember thinking about it at the time. It could only have been that they had been so anxious to dispose of the body as soon as they had the opportunity to do so. That chance had presented itself unexpectedly when they crossed the bridge at Bothwell on their way back to Carlisle. Having first tied the body to a lump of concrete which they had found in a bombed building nearby, they dropped the corpse into the river from the bridge. There had been no traffic to speak of on the road at that late hour, and fortunately it had been a very dark night. They had parked their vehicle close to the bridge, knowing that it would not have been given a second glance by anyone passing by, because people had been so used to seeing army transport on the road. Even if any other vehicle had passed by at the time it would be almost impossible to connect their vehicle with the murder, as the police had stated in the newspapers that they didn't know exactly when the body was dumped. Andy felt certain that he couldn't be traced. Later that afternoon he had an unexpected visitor.

Private Sidney Cope stood at the bottom of Andy's bed looking very serious.

"What the hell are you doing here, Sid? I thought we'd agreed nae to be seen together."

"I found out where you were from your neighbour in the tenement block. She told me that you'd had to go into the hospital again. I've had a job finding out which bloody hospital."

"You hinna been roon' to my flat you silly sod!? We're nae supposed to ken one another!"

Sidney dismissed Andy's rebuke. "But have you seen the papers? They've found that bloody American."

Andy looked round to see if anyone had heard him. "Why don't you keep your damn voice doon? Do you want the whole ward to hear you? I've seen the story and I dinna ken what you're worried aboot. Anyway, who's going to tell the polis' aboot anything? Charlie won't split. He'll lose his diamonds if he did, and I'm jist waiting to spend that money which I hinna even touched yet."

"Don't be stupid," Sid remarked. "Have you forgotten about that girl of Joe's that you twisted out of her fortune? What's she got to lose if she tells the police about what Joe was carrying. If she's got any brains, she'll put two and two together and realise that you've pinched the money, and now that Joe's body's been found, presume that you killed him."

Andy jumped in quickly before Sid could say any more. "If she finds out what happened at Charlie's place, the polis' will question Charlie 'til they get the truth, and then you'll be in trouble."

"The best thing you can do is to get out of here as soon as you can, and disappear," Sid said.

"Why should I dae that? I didna kill Joe, you did!"

It was now Sid's turn to look around in case anyone else was listening. "And you're an accomplice and don't you forget it, chum. When are you likely to get out of this bloody hole?"

"When they tell me. The doctor's coming today to tell me what's happening. I'm beginning to get some feeling in my fingers again."

"You'll get some feeling in your bloody neck when the rope is round it if we're not careful. I think we'd better lie low until this thing blows over. Tell that quack of yours that you want to go home, and then we'll get together and sort this thing out."

After his unwelcome visitor had left, Andy worried about his half of the money that he had hidden in his flat. He knew Sid too well to be able to trust him. He had to get out of the hospital as quickly as possible.

CHAPTER FOURTEEN

Inspector Alistair McIntosh went over the papers in the case of Joe Peabody's murder yet again, still not sure whether he had all the information he wanted. He waited patiently for his sergeant to arrive with Howard Hartwell and Elizabeth Harrison. The war department had sent the inspector the information he had requested about Andy McKern, together with details about the wound to his arm, and that he had been told to attend the Royal Infirmary in Glasgow for treatment. However, when enquiries had been made at the hospital the previous evening, it was found that he had discharged himself a couple of days earlier, nor was he at the Glasgow address they had been given by the hospital. The police had also been supplied with the name of another soldier who had been stationed at the same Barracks as McKern, and who had the same address in Carlisle as him. Following the police request for information as to the movements of these men in around January they had discovered that this other soldier had been used an army vehicle to take some things to a depot in Glasgow, returning the following day. The inspector looked again at the papers and read the name Private Sidney Cope. He didn't think he needed to pursue this, as he considered that this other soldier would be nothing to do with his inquiry. His mind was on the two people his sergeant was bringing in.

Howard and Liz came into his room followed by Sergeant Baillie. The inspector was taken aback when he saw how pretty she was. He smiled, and, unusually for him at first, was lost for words. He then found his voice. "So we meet at last, Miss Harrison."

"I didn't think I was so important that you needed to seek me out."

"Well, there are some questions I'd like to ask you with regard to this inquiry and into the circumstances of this American soldier's death."

"I see," she said coolly.

"Apart from just being a fellow traveller on the train, you knew this Joe Peabody, didn't you?"

"I did."

The inspector was silent for a moment. He had expected her to deny it. He shuffled through the papers on his desk and selected a document which he waved at her. "But you told the Carlisle police when they questioned you in January, that he was only someone who you'd seen on the train, and that your boyfriend was this man," he pointed to Howard.

"Well, that wasn't quite right. I had known Joe for some months, and when he came back from Europe he told me that he had to see someone in Scotland. He had apparently arranged for a soldier he'd met on the boat coming over, to book a room in a hotel in Glasgow, and we'd have a few nights together. I didn't love Joe but he always excited me."

The sergeant was smiling at her all this time. He wouldn't have minded a bit of excitement with her himself, he thought. He heard the inspector's voice booming at him.

"Sergeant, are you making a note of all this?" Then, turning back to the girl, he said with a sarcastic tone in his voice, "Go on, your story is fascinating."

Sergeant Baillie glared at his inspector and thought how unkindly he had spoken to her. Liz was glad of the break. Although she had rehearsed this story with Howard, it gave her time to think what she was saying and to get the rest of the story right. Most of it was true anyway.

"I suspected that he'd come over without permission, or whatever it's called, and when Howard and I saw Joe being arrested - or who we thought was Joe - the last thing I wanted to do was to get involved. After talking it over with Howard," she turned towards him and squeezed his hand - "he was marvellous to me by the way - I decided to change the name in the register to Howard's name and pretend that he was my husband. After a few days I was lonely, so I went to the camp and arranged to meet him, and you probably know the rest."

The inspector was listening very carefully to everything she had to say. "Go on," he said. He was half beginning to believe her story and wanted to see if it tallied with what they'd already found out.

"Well, we spent Tuesday night together and arranged to have another night, but we had a disagreement..." Sergeant Baillie thought that he noticed her bottom lip tremble a little, "and I....." Liz tried to continue and managed to find a tear and let it run down her cheek. "I'm sorry, Inspector, but now that we've found each other again, we've fallen in love, and I really don't want to talk about that time when I left him in the lurch in January. I thought he would hate me for it at the time, but he's forgiven me now." She wiped the tear from her cheek with her finger.

The sergeant was already close by her side and handed her his handkerchief to dry her eyes.

The inspector became a little agitated, None of this was leading him any nearer to solving the murder. He wasn't fully convinced that the girl was telling him the truth, but now he wanted to know how Howard had acquired that diamond.

"Mr. Hartwell, we've since discovered that you paid the Bill at the hotel with a diamond. I would like you to tell me....."

The door to his office opened abruptly, and a young officer stood there, "Sorry to interrupt you, sir, but some very important information has just been 'phoned through in regard to this case you are investigating. I thought that you should know."

The inspector looked towards the two he had been questioning as he prepared to leave the room. "You will excuse me. I'll be back in a minute."

"Now, what is it, officer? What's so important? I'm in the middle of a murder enquiry."

"I'm aware of that, sir, but the body of that soldier you wanted to interview has been found in a flat in a tenement building."

Inspector McIntosh went back into the room and turned to Liz and Howard. "You can go for the present, but I'll want to talk to you both again," then, walking briskly to the door, he grabbed his sergeant's arm. "Right Baillie, we're going visiting." He explained to his sergeant where they were going when they were in the car. "I think I now know who, but I'm damned if I know why!" he added.

When they arrived at the building, a sole policeman stood at the open door of the flat. McKern lay face down on the floor in a crumpled heap. The room was in state of untidiness. Drawers were open and the contents strewn about all over the place.

"Looks as if he's been robbed," Sergeant Baillie observed, "unless the murderer was looking for something in particular. What do you think, sir?"

Alistair ignored the question, but turned the officer on duty, "Who found the body?"

"It was the lady next door, sir. She saw the door open when she came to go out shopping. She doesn't remember hearing anything, but said that she was a little deaf. There's no blood, sir, so I think he must have been struck down..."

Alistair interrupted him, "Thank you officer: we'll leave the analysis to the experts if you don't mind." More police arrived and then the pathologist. Turning to his sergeant added, "Nothing else we can do here, Baillie, we'll leave so that they can get on with doing what they have to do. Meanwhile, lets get back to the station. I want you to make a couple of telephone calls."

He looked towards the pathologist. "I expect you won't be long here. After you've got this laddie back, I'll see you at the hospital in about an hour or so. Is that enough time for you?"

"Yes I think so. Looks pretty straight forward to me. Reckon he died about midnight."

An hour-and-a-half later, Inspector McIntosh was at the hospital mortuary talking to the pathologist.

"You're making a habit of these kind of corpses, Alistair? This is the second one you've given me inside a fortnight with the same cause of death."

"Strangled? the inspector asked.

"Well, sort of. I believe that the cause of death was the same as the last one, but this one's easier to detect as he's only been dead since about midnight as I told you at the flat; not bloated like the last one, you see. This one died as a result of cardiac shock from compression of the neck ganglia."

"You mean strangled!" repeated the inspector.

"Well, it's not quite the same but it'll do. The important thing is that someone would have to know exactly what to do to kill a man in this way."

"Do you think the same person did both murders?"

"Could be. He'd have to be someone who knew exactly how to do it. It's most unusual. It's just a question of making sure he got the right place on the neck to exert the pressure. If I had to guess, I would say he's probably a soldier who's been trained to kill."

"Well you leave the guessing to me, but I thought it might be," Alistair remarked.

"By the way, Alistair, did you hear that we found a one-hundred pound note under the body."

As the inspector made his way back to the station, he knew now that it had been a case of robbery, but a one-hundred pound note was an awful lot of money, and there must have been more in the flat. He wondered what his sergeant would have to tell him from the telephone calls he had asked him to make.

When he arrived at the station, Sergeant Baillie followed him into his room. "You were quite right, sir. That friend of the deceased, Corporal Cope, is on a three days' leave. He's due back later today. I also rang the hospital like you said, and they told me that McKern had a visitor the day before yesterday. He fitted the description of Cope which was given to me by the camp."

"Did you tell them to detain him when he gets back, and that we want to question him?"

Baillie nodded. "If he did both the murders, then what was his motive?"

"Robbery I think, but we'll have to wait to find out when we arrest him."

"Arrest him? Does that mean we'll be going all the way to Carlisle, sir?"

"That's why I asked you to make that third telephone call, Sergeant. What did you find out?"

"There is a slow train at five o'clock, or there's the overnight express to London which stops at Carlisle, and leaves at nine, otherwise we'll have to wait until tomorrow morning."

"Well done, Baillie. It all depends when we hear from the Commanding Officer at the Barracks."

Later that afternoon, the inspector received a telephone call from the Camp Commandant of the Army Camp at Carlisle.

"Major Corkingdale here, Inspector. I'm afraid I have some bad news for you. That Corporal Cope you wanted to question. Dead, I'm afraid. Silly ass went berserk when we told him that you wanted to question him about a murder. Snatched a loaded gun from one of the MPs and tried to commandeer an army staff car. One of the MPs shot at him to wound him, and to try and prevent him from getting away, but missed his aim I'm afraid, and shot him straight through the heart. Quite accidental, of course. There'll be a stink about it. Shouldn't have done it, naturally, but he reacted quickly when he saw the gun pointing at him. Very sorry, Inspector, but I do have some good news for you."

Inspector Alistair McIntosh couldn't believe his ears. His only suspect dead! What news could there be that was good? "What's the good news?" he asked, feeling completely dejected.

"Found almost £34,000 in old notes in a bag he was carrying. All large notes. An absolute fortune! No doubt that's why he didn't want to be arrested and tried to get away. Is that what you wanted him for, Inspector? Did he rob a bank or something and kill someone in the process? He was trained for it. One of our best men at one time, mark you. Such a lot of money. What do you want me to do with it? God! What a mess!"

Alistair was lost for words. £34,000! He had to think. "Can I call you back, Major? I'll try and tell you what's to be done as soon as I've consulted my Chief."

Alistair knew that his Chief Superintendent would have to be told all about this, but first, he thought that he had better try and sort it out. There was now no point in dashing off to Carlisle, and Cope had confirmed his suspicions that he had murdered his friend McKern by trying to run away when he was told why he was wanted for questioning. The money he had in his possession, which he had no doubt stolen from McKern after he had killed him, was yet another reason for running away, and solved his problem about motive - but how did Andy McKern have all that money? £34,000 was, after all, an awful lot! If Cope had also killed the American before dumping him into the Clyde, it was probably because Joe Peabody had the money in the first place.

"Well, Baillie, what do you think?" Alistair looked closely at his sergeant after telling him all that the Major had told him.

Sergeant Baillie was an uncomplicated man with simple needs. He wasn't even able to imagine what £34,000 looked like. He had no idea where that amount of money could have come from, or why it had been in that soldier's flat.

"Do you think he might have been holding it for somebody, sir? If the money was his own, surely he would have cleared off before this."

"I didn't want you to ask me what I thought, but you have made an important observation, Sergeant. Perhaps he was waiting to see if the operations on his arm were successful before disappearing, but go on, think, man."

"The girl might know more than she has told us already, sir? If she knew that the American was carrying money for McKern, then she wouldn't have admitted it for fear of incriminating herself."

"Now you're getting warm, Sergeant. Remember the American, Joseph Peabody, was killed in the same way as Andy McKern."

"Of course, sir. Perhaps McKern knew that the American had the money and told his pal, Cope, who killed him. McKern kept the money safe until he came out of hospital, but Cope murdered him...no, sir, that can't be right. Why was there any need to kill anybody? And if the American was carrying all that money, where was he taking it to?"

"You've confirmed my theory, Baillie. I think we've got the story about right, but not the details, and there are still a few questions left unanswered. Let's have that girl in again with Hartwell. Mind you, I don't think the Navy fellow had anything to do with it. I suspect that she picked him up on the train as a substitute for her American boyfriend, who she thought had been arrested."

When Liz and Howard returned to the police station they were both very nervous and apprehensive as to what questions they were going to be asked. Howard had thought up what he considered to be an answer to the inspector's inevitable question of where he had obtained the diamond which he had sold at the hotel. However, the inspector began by asking Liz a different question. He thrust a one-hundred pound note across the table towards her. "What do know about this?"

Liz immediately guessed that it was from the money that had been paid in exchange for the diamonds. "Nothing. I've never seen a one-hundred pound note before. Where did you get it?" she asked, trying to sound innocent of any knowledge about the money.

"That Scottish soldier friend of your American has also been found strangled here in Glasgow. The note was found in his flat where he had been murdered."

"Surely you don't think that we..."

The inspector interrupted her. "No, Miss Harrison. We know that neither of you were involved. However, we're pretty certain that we know who the murderer was, but there has been a lot of money stolen, and we're trying to find out where it all came from. Do you think that your late friend, G.I.Joe Peabody, might have been carrying some money when you were travelling with him on the train in January?"

The inspector's question had told her that the police knew nothing about the diamonds, and although she had gasped at the news of the soldier's murder, she wasn't too upset. His death would mean that there was one less to worry about who knew about the diamonds.

"Now you've mentioned it, Sergeant, he did tell me he had to pay some money to someone in Glasgow, and I've just remembered that he took his case with him when he got off the train at Carlisle. It must have contained the money you are talking about. We didn't find anything that he'd left on the train, did we, Howard? I'd never thought about that until you just reminded me of it."

Howard was confused as he listened to Liz lying to the police officers, but found himself nodding in agreement at her answer to his question. She must know what she is doing, he thought, and her story sounded so believable. The inspector leaned across the table, picked up the note and waved in front of her face. "And who was he taking it to did he say? Was it that soldier?"

"That's the trouble, Inspector. If he had told us where he had been taking it, we would have remembered about the money before now. So - I'm afraid - the answer is... We don't know."

The inspector sat very still, staring at her, trying to read into her eyes whether or not she was telling the truth. After what seemed to Liz to be an eternity, he leaned back in his chair smiling to himself. He could see no reason for questioning either of them any further. He suspected that she was lying about something, but he was convinced that they had nothing to do with the murders. "Right, you can both go now. I doubt if I'll need to see you again."

Howard grabbed Liz firmly by the arm as he hurried her out of the building.

"What's the rush, Howard? Where are you taking me?"

"It was that one-hundred pound note which reminded me," Howard said excitedly. "Have you forgotten that MacKenzie offered us five-hundred pounds each if we told the police nothing - and we haven't, so let's go and pick up that money before it's too late."

Inspector McIntosh couldn't wait to call his sergeant back into his office. "I think I've got it," he announced. "Listen to me Sergeant and tell me if I've got it wrong."

"Before you start, sir, I took another call from that Major at the camp. He said that they've searched Corporal Cope's things and found another huge sum of money. Another twenty-odd thousand pounds!"

The inspector raised both of his hands, and looked relieved. "Good man, Baillie. You've just supplied the missing link. There's no doubt in my mind that Cope did both murders. The motive was the old one - greed. I believe that the American had originally planned to take the money to Glasgow to McKern to purchase something, or to pass on to someone else, meeting him at Carlisle as had been arranged previously without telling Miss Harrison. He obviously intended to re-board the train and carry on to Glasgow with his girl friend. For some reason he didn't do it. It may have been the incident that happened on the platform when that other U.S. soldier was arrested, or McKern had been late turning up, or for some other reason. We'll never know, but whatever it was, McKern intended to keep the money for himself, and arranged with his friend to probably kidnap Joe, kill him later and share the money between them. Remember, McKern couldn't do much with that arm so he had to have help. Perhaps they are the reasons why he never got back on the train. After all, the opportunity presented itself very conveniently when that other soldier was arrested. Everyone would be preoccupied with that and not notice what else was going on."

The sergeant interrupted his inspector, anxious to show that he was following his hypothesis. "And then the following week, Cope used an Army vehicle to take some supplies to Glasgow, and probably used it to carry their victim's body to Bothwell."

"That's right, Sergeant, glad that you're paying attention. After murdering the American, they carried him the army truck and dumped him in the Clyde where no one would be able to find him. Alright so far, Sergeant?"

"Can't find fault with that yet, sir."

"With the message you've just received, it appears that Cope had his share hidden away, and the one-hundred pound note we found in McKern's flat confirms that he must have had his money there. Whatever they, or Cope on his own had planned was held up because of McKern's operation on his arm, but as soon as he came out of hospital, Cope suddenly took it into his head to take Andy's share by murdering him, return to the camp to pick up the rest of the cash and then disappear."

"But we rumbled him, and he was caught when he returned to the camp," the sergeant concluded. "But where did all that money come from in the first place, sir? Even if Joe Peabody had brought it with him on the train.

"We'll never know that either, Sergeant, unless you'd like to start a separate investigation when I've taken my pension, but remember, the only people who could have told you are now all dead!"

Inspector Alistair McIntosh rose from his chair, looking very pleased with himself. "I think I'd better go and see the Chief now, and you can start on the report, Sergeant."

"Er, just before you go, Inspector..." Sergeant Baillie rarely addressed Alistair as Inspector, and he stopped dead in his tracks. It was almost as though he was being questioned about a serious error of judgement he had made.

"What is it, Baillie?"

"Where did Hartwell say he got that diamond?"

Alistair suddenly realised that when he had begun to see the conclusion of this, his last case, he'd forgotten to ask the sailor about it. "Oh that?" the inspector was searching to find a plausible excuse. "Oh that?" he repeated, "Does it really matter, It can't be anything to do with the case, and I can't afford to start on another enquiry. I'm retiring, Sergeant, had you forgotten?"

ANNIE

It had been eight years since Annie's husband had died, and during that time she had been able to manage very well all on her own. But now, at eighty-six years of age, she found that the house was much too big for her, and looking after it and doing all the shopping herself was getting her down. Her three children were married with families, and all were a long way away; consequently she saw little of them. Although she had lived in the same town, and the same house for over sixty years, she was beginning to see less and less of her friends, so she thought that it would be a nice idea to be re-united with her remaining sisters who lived close to each other, albeit in a different town. All three were younger than her.

One was a widow who lived on her own, but the other two were single and had always been so. As so many young men were killed between 1914 and 1918, they always boasted, somewhat amusingly, to be the 'unclaimed jewels of the 1st World War'.

Annie made the decision to pay them a visit, but when she arrived she found that Mary, the youngest one, was in a Nursing Home. Nevertheless, Annie quickly saw the advantages of being in such a place, and decided there and then that she would join her if at all possible. The Nursing Home not only appealed to her, but seeing her sister being so well looked after, she thought that it would be the ideal way to spend the remaining years of her life. In addition, she discovered that her other two sisters visited the Home every day, so she would have their company as well as Mary's.

Annie returned home and set about making the arrangements. She gave up the house and booked into the same Nursing Home as her sister, and in a very short time moved in with her. Soon she became quite content in doing little else but reading and having long conversations with Mary, and looked forward to the visits by her other two sisters each day.

Things went well at first, and then poor Mary had a stroke, and any communication with her was impossible. A year later she died, and the daily visits that Annie had enjoyed from her other two sisters became less frequent. During the next two or three months, she saw very little of them, and it wasn't long before she felt lonely again and unhappy there. Her youngest son, Harry, and his wife, Margaret, seeing how gloomy she had become, suggested that they would find a Nursing Home close to where they themselves lived, so that they could visit her regularly and attend to all her needs.

Annie seemed happy with this arrangement, and was even able to enjoy visits from her grandchildren. However, after two or three years there, she suddenly aged, and began to require full nursing attention which the dedicated staff were able to give. Fortunately, apart from some deafness and failing eyesight, her general health was good and, although suffering from some loss of memory, she remained sound of mind and aware of her surroundings until the last day of her life, four months after reaching her ninety-fifth birthday.

Sadly, a number of the ladies in the home were not so lucky, many suffering from senile-dementure. Annie had little patience with them, and somewhat unkindly often remarked in far too loud a voice, "They're nearly all mad in here!"

Sometimes she would be amused by what had happened and

relate the incidents to Harry and Margaret when they visited. "Maudy was 90 yesterday," she told them on one occasion. "I asked her what she was going to do and she said that she was going into town with her mother! She often sits there all day talking to herself. Last night she wandered into someone else's room and put Mabel's teeth in by mistake."

Annie always saw the funny side of these sort of things and had a good laugh about them. During the last year of her life, however, she found it difficult to find the right words to describe what she really wanted. Although she was aware that the word she had said wasn't the one she had meant to say, it sometimes became quite amusing for Harry and Margaret to help her to try and find the right one.

On one occasion when her son went to see her, she asked if he'd brought the bubble-gum. She pointed in the direction of the kitchen. "I keep asking them in there for it, but they never bring it to me. Have YOU brought me some?"

Harry smiled at the thought of his ninety-four year old mother chewing bubble-gum. "But you don't like bubble-gum, mother." He also remembered how she hated him to have it when he was a child.

"Spit it out," she had said angrily when he had been foolish enough to let his mother catch him with some spearmint, "it'll stick to your inside, and probably kill you," she had added with conviction. It was a belief she held all her life, so it was incomprehensible that she was asking for it now.

"I don't think you mean bubble-gum mother. Are you sure you mean bubble-gum?"

"No!" she said in exasperation, "Not bubble-gum." She shook her head and closed her eyes tightly, wrestling with her thoughts, and trying to speak the words she had really meant to say. "I don't know what I mean. I can't find the right word." She sighed, and looked annoyed with herself.

"Do you mean your hearing-aid?" Harry suggested hopefully. She often talked about her hearing-aids. She had two. Sometimes she couldn't get either of them to work properly and fiddled with them constantly. Often it was because the batteries had run down, but she always blamed the appliances. The trouble was, her hearing was getting worse, and when the thing in her ear whistled she was the only one who couldn't hear it!

"Just a minute," she would say when she noticed that someone was speaking to her, and then fiddle with the control on the ear piece to try and get it right.

Even when the volume was turned up as far as it would go, she became quite agitated when she couldn't hear what people were saying, and then, in exasperation, announce, "Oh I can't get this silly thing to work. I think that the battery must have gone again."

Harry repeated the question he had asked, this time speaking very much louder. "MOTHER, DO YOU MEAN YOUR HEARING-AID?"

She heard him this time, even without the thing stuck in her ear.

"No, I don't mean my hearing-aid," she answered impatiently.

He tried other things that she frequently asked for by mouthing them so that she could read his lips. "Talcum-powder? toilet-paper? pencil? calendar?"

She shook her head at all his suggestions. There was a moment's silence: she was thinking, then asked him the same question again as if he had only just arrived. "Have you brought the bubble-gum?" She nodded towards the door. "I keep asking them in there to bring it but they don't bother. They don't care."

"They do care, mother. They look after you very well, but there are others in here too, that need looking after."

"Not as much as me." She looked quite hurt that her son didn't understand that she considered that her needs were greater than others. "Would you go and ask them to bring my bubble-gum?"

Harry was beginning to give up, but thankfully, at that moment he was joined by his wife. Margaret was much closer to his own mother than he was, and always appeared to have a better understanding of her needs than anyone else. Before there was any chance to exchange greetings, Annie asked her, "Have you brought my bubble-gum? I'm having my bath this afternoon and I'll need it!"

Margaret knew immediately what she wanted and took the large bottle containing pink liquid from out of the bag she was carrying, and held it up triumphantly. Her mother-in-law gave her a big smile.

"Oh, you mean BUBBLE-BATH," Harry drawled, feeling a sense of relief that it had all been sorted out at long last. Then laughed to himself at the thought of his mother having a bath in bubble-gum!

"That's what I said - bubble-gum," she said, then turning again to her daughter-in-law asked her what it was for.

"It's for making the water nice when you have your bath," Margaret explained simply.

"I know THAT," Annie retorted, "but what is it for?"

Margaret told her again but got the same response, so she gave up and changed the subject.

"What did you have for dinner today?"

"Meat, potatoes, and cabbage."

"And pudding?"

Annie thought about it for a second or two as if trying to remember, and then as the light dawned said enthusiastically, "Oh it was something rather special." Then her facial expression changed as she really remembered what it was. "Well, it was quite ordinary really - something all messed up."

Margaret thought it best not to pursue that subject any further.

"Would you bring this up to date for me?" she was trying to open Margaret's handbag.

"No, that's mine," Margaret said kindly, and then gave her her own bulging one which wasn't even fastened.

Annie rummaged around inside for a while then took out a large tatty and torn calendar. It was even more dilapidated than the last time they had seen it. As long as Harry could remember, she had always had a calendar on which she crossed out the date of each day as it came, tearing off the months as they went by. She always knew the day and the date but, during the last few months for the first time in her life, it had been neglected. It was now May, and April was still there with only a few days crossed out.

Margaret tore out the April page. "We'll throw that away to start with. April has gone, and I'll cross off the days to the 19th May," and then, pointing to the twentieth, said, "That is tomorrow!"

"Oh yes," Annie said knowingly, "that's Monday," and trying to sound as though she had known it all along.

"No it's not," Margaret said, trying not to hurt her feelings, "it's Saturday!" and then, as she saw the look of disappointment on her mother-in-law's face, wished that she hadn't said anything. "But it doesn't really matter," she added quickly, "I'll look at it again the next time I come and keep it up-to-date for you." She leant forward and kissed her on the cheek. Harry did the same then they both took their leave.

Sometimes the conversations Harry and Margaret had with his mother during their visits didn't always go smoothly.

"Hello, mum,"

"Oh hello. You're late!"

"No we're not late, we're early. We're going out this afternoon, so we thought we'd come to see you before you have your lunch, so we're early."

"No you're not. You're late!"

"How can we be late, we don't usually come to see you in the mornings."

"Well, you haven't much time. We have our lunch at twelve."

"We know that. It's only half-past eleven."

There was a long pause after that, but then the couple wished that they hadn't had the final word. She looked so disappointed that they had won the argument. They waited for the inevitable to happen.

Annie stared straight ahead, deliberately not looking in their direction. "I don't feel well," she said, trying to gain their sympathy.

"Why not? What's the matter?"

"It's my ears. Mr. Hainton (he was the proprietor of the Nursing Home), is going to take them to the hospital for me this afternoon."

Harry tried to controlled himself from making the obvious remark. What she had said reminded him of the old joke about the sign, "Ear Piercing While You Wait."

"Mr Hainton is taking your hearing-aids to the hospital, you mean?"

His Mother didn't bother to respond to that. Unfortunately, she had not got the sympathy she had been seeking. She'd have to try something else.

"My tummy's playing up."

"Where does it hurt," Harry asked. He realised immediately that it had been a stupid question, and the look she gave him confirmed that it had been.

"Here," she said pointing to her midriff, with a little too much emphasis he thought.

Anxious to change the subject, Harry said cheerfully, "It's nice and warm in here."

"I'm cold."

Margaret thought that she'd have a try. "We've been to quite a number of parties over Christmas."

"What do you want to go to parties for? They'll be coming to fetch me soon for my meal."

121

"There's still ten minutes to go yet, mother." They began to realise that she probably had had enough of them. Perhaps she didn't like them coming in the morning, or maybe she was getting impatient wondering whether they might be holding her up from her lunch. A voice behind them lightened the atmosphere.

"Did I come to the party?"

It was the old lady whom they had noticed had been asleep when they arrived. She had been a Headmistress of a Private School, but now, sadly, she didn't know where she was or even the time of day.

"No, Miss Plumrose. You stayed here." Harry tried to say it as kindly as he could.

"I wouldn't be able to get in and out of the car." She said slowly and very quietly, and sounding very disappointed.

"Never mind, Miss Plumrose, perhaps another time." Harry's remark brought no response, but then looked more closely at her and noticed that she had gone back to sleep.

Suddenly Annie said, "Thank you for coming," and reached out to pull the cord with the red knob on the end. "I think I want to go to the toilet before my meal."

They gave her the usual kiss, and a little wave as they left the room.

It wasn't unusual for other residents to join in with the conversations between Annie and her son and his wife. Because of her deafness and the usual trouble with her hearing aid, they often had to speak rather loudly to her. This gave one or two of the other residents nearby the belief that they were talking to them. Some had very few, if any, visitors, and for that reason the couple didn't mind whether the other ladies joined in with their conversation, but Harry's mother wasn't too pleased when they did.

On one particular Christmas day, they had taken some flowers to give her, together with a lovely poinsettia in a pot.

"We've already got one of those," she said, pointing to a much larger one in the hearth.

She told them that she had had some toiletries as presents but didn't want them. They noticed that Miss Plumrose was asleep as usual.

"I don't need them. You can take them away," Annie said quite firmly.

"No, mother. They're presents for you, and you'll need them when you've used up the others you have. We'll put them in your drawer."

She leaned forward and fiddled with her hearing aid. "What did you say, I can't hear you. It's never been the same since I went to the hospital with it. Mr. Hainton tried to get it to go but it still keeps going funny."

"I SAID I'LL PUT THEM IN YOUR DRAWER," Harry said in a much louder voice.

Miss Plumrose opened her eyes. "What have you put in my drawer?"

Annie was still fiddling with her hearing aid and showed no reaction to what Harry had said. "IN YOUR DRAWER," they both shouted again holding the things up for her to see.

"Which drawer?" asked Miss Plumrose.

"Not you, Miss Plumrose," Margaret said with understanding. "Happy Christmas to you."

"Is it Christmas?"

Annie suddenly remembered that her daughter, Dorothy, had sent her some flowers.

"Were they in a box?" Harry asked.

"No. They were from the Channel Isles." and then as an afterthought, his mother said, "I've never been there."

"Neither have I," said Eva. She was another lady sitting on the other side of the room.

Her friend, Edna, who was sitting next to Eva and stroking a cat on her lap, said, "I don't even know where it is."

As Harry and Margaret left, they were confronted by another resident who was wandering aimlessly about between two of the rooms. "Can I have a word with you?" she said, beckoning to them. "I wonder if you can you tell me where I am."

It was early one morning almost a year afterwards when Harry received a telephone call from Mr Hainton at the Home. "Annie," he said, "had just fallen asleep and the doctor thought that she'd probably had a stroke."

Harry sat with her for a while holding her hand, but she never woke again and passed away peacefully the following night.

MRS. LEYTON

Jim Walker was a family man. He had joined a Life Assurance Company as a young man, did well as a District Agent, and was then promoted to Assistant District Manager. His reputation with dealing with the opposite sex was well known, and whenever a difficult situation developed, the staff knew that they could call on Jim to sort it all out satisfactorily. He had a way of smoothing things over until the "awkward customer" had almost to apologise to him.

On one such occasion, he was standing talking to the girl clerks, when he noticed a lady just inside the door, hesitating and appearing to be very reluctant to come to the counter.

"Can I help you?" he asked. She strode towards him, now with more confidence.

"Well yes, I hope so."

Joe's experience told him that she was going to ask a difficult question. As she looked straight at him, he couldn't help noticing her butterfly-winged spectacles. They looked expensive: very large with floral frames, and with long pointed spikes at the top which protruded way outside her temples. He thought that they must have either have cost a lot of money, or she'd had them out of a Christmas cracker!

"I want to insure my spectacles," she said calmly.

Jim began to explain, "They can be covered under the All Risks section of your Household Insurance. What do you...."

She interrupted him, "No! no, I don't want to insure them. I want to insure against anyone else having a pair like them!"

Jim's first thought was that no one in their right mind could possibly own a similar pair to those she was wearing, but thought that it would be unkind to say so. For a moment he was speechless. It was almost unheard of for Jim to be lost for words.

"Er, Why? What do you mean?" It was the best he could do. He thought he heard a stifled snigger from one of the girls behind him, and clenched a fist in an effort to control himself.

"Well it's like this," she continued, "I'm a schoolteacher..."

Jim thought that she was perfect for that role. Possibly an English teacher and a spinster. She looked the part when she stood waiting by the door in her flat soled shoes, knee-length tweed skirt and woollen twin-set, and wearing a single row of pearls. She fiddled with the shoulder-strap of her brown leather hand-bag as she spoke.

She continued, "...and last year I had a dress made exclusively for me. The shop confirmed that the material was a 'one-off', but imagine my consternation when I returned to school after the summer holidays, and wearing the dress - to see a colleague with a belt made out of the same material! I was livid, especially when she told me that she had bought it from Marks and Spencers of all places!"

Jim noticed that her eyes looked fiery through those large ornate spectacles.

"So now," she continued, firmly and positively, "I've spent a lot of money on these spectacles, and although I have had the assurance from the optician that they are unique, I want to insure against my colleague, er - someone - anyone - having a pair similar!"

So the truth was out. A slip of her tongue had revealed the jealousy between her colleague and herself. Jim used all his diplomatic expertise to explain that unfortunately there wasn't any way that he could help her with that type of insurance. Perhaps she could try Lloyds of London, he suggested, or obtain a much firmer assurance from her optician. She thanked him politely, and as she closed the door, the office exploded with laughter which had been miraculously suppressed all the while the lady had been explaining her plight and requirements.

Jim was also a man with strong morals, but these had been tested on more than one occasion when calling on his policyholders in their own homes. It would have been very easy for him to have an affair or two with some of the ladies he visited, and had to steel himself from the temptations sometimes offered. However, his reputation and status in the company always bore him in good stead, and prevented him for straying from the straight and narrow, except that on one particular occasion a call on a policyholder nearly led to his downfall.

A very smart lady came into the office one day as Jim stood talking to the office clerks. She caused heads to turn as soon this extremely attractive, tall and elegant lady walked towards the counter.

"Oh! my favourite man," she screeched, recognising Jim. He felt the colour rush quickly to his cheeks.

"Oh hello, Mrs Leyton." He tried to make his greeting sound quite normal, but was aware that everyone had stopped working, they were all silent waiting to hear every word that she had to say.

She gave Jim a radiant smile. "I was in all day on Monday and wondered where you were! I thought I saw you in the Close, but you didn't call, and I especially wanted you."

The staff in the office immediately began to misinterpret the meaning of the phrase she had used, and Jim, being aware of this, felt himself going redder and redder. The Manager walked back into his own office but left the door open so that he could hear every word that was being said. He wasn't going to miss any of this.

Jim's mouth felt dry; he opened it to speak but the words took some time to come. The lady was looking at him with her alert, big green eyes, above a dusting of ginger and light-brown facial freckles. He felt very hot, and beads of sweat began forming on his forehead as he remembered their last meeting at her home four weeks previously. It seemed a long time before he replied but, eventually, after clearing his throat, the words came.

"I didn't think you were going to be in at that time. I intended to call back but it slipped my memory," he lied. It sounded such a feeble explanation. The truth was that he deliberately hadn't called, but couldn't tell her so. They stood facing each other across the counter, her beautiful red hair and freckled face giving her an almost child-like appearance. He dared not look again into those wide open eyes, and instead fixed his gaze on her tiny freckled nose, the tip turned up slightly, as if the shape had been designed especially for her. She gave him another smile as she took the premium books from her handbag and handed them to him. He knew from her expression that she had not believed a word he had said.

"Would you take the payment due for the next four weeks as well - you've got last month's to put down, you remember." He glanced up and their eyes met for a split second, and was sure that she gave him a little wink. He remembered very well. How could he forget.

"I'll be moving to Birmingham in a couple of weeks time as I'm getting married again."

Her announcement took him completely by surprise. She had said it all so matter of fact and devoid of any expression. He just gave a little "Oh!" immediately, feeling disappointed when he realised that the incident of four weeks ago would not be repeated. Perhaps it was all for the best.

Just then the telephone rang, sounding much louder than usual in the silent office. It was answered by one of the girl clerks.

"Excuse me, Mr. Walker, you're wanted on the telephone."

Jim apologised to the lady and turned to the senior clerk. "Would you deal with Mrs. Leyton for me, Sheila?"

The call was only brief, and one that Jim had been expecting, confirming an appointment. He saw that Sheila was deep in conversation with Mrs Leyton, probably about her forthcoming marriage so, after replacing the receiver, he stayed by the telephone staring out of the window....

Jim had always looked forward to calling on Mrs. Leyton in the village of Hilltone.

"Her husband's left her," the district agent, Frank Jackson, had told him when they had gone to the house for the first time, "heaven knows why - she's gorgeous." He rubbed his hands together hunching his shoulders as his imagination ran away with him.

When she answered the door, Jim had known exactly what his colleague meant. She wasn't just beautiful, she was sex personified. Her red hair and freckled face gave her a youthful and innocent appearance, but her shapely figure underneath the very short thin dress she was wearing left little to the imagination. Even at this first meeting, she had confided in Jim, telling him how lonely she felt being separated from her husband. She did explain that he sent her money, but with her little six year old girl to look after, she hardly ever went out. Jim was happily married, but if he hadn't been it would have been a different story. All the wrong thoughts came into his head.

"She's too good for you," Jim had quipped to Frank as they left the house, "much too sophisticated."

This had been about two years ago, but she had had such an effect on Jim that he made every excuse to call whenever he was working with the agent in her area. She talked freely to him about her life, and he felt a strong physical attraction to her. Her mini skirts seemed to get even shorter with each visit revealing even more of her long shapely legs. She always appeared pleased to see him, and Jim was often thankful that the agent always went with him to the house, as he was sure that if he had made an advance towards her, she would have welcomed it, and that would have been the undoing of him.

Then a couple of months ago, the District Agent had left the Company. When Jim called in her village, he had chosen very carefully and deliberately the time he called at her house, having first calculated that her little girl would be at school for another two hours. Mrs Leyton greeted him enthusiastically, even excitedly he thought. She was wearing only a thin blouse which showed the contours of her well shaped breasts, and she had on the briefest mini which revealed most of her bare thighs. Jim suddenly felt strangely nervous, especially when she invited him into the lounge to sit down while she looked for the premium books. Unsure of himself, he chose to remain in the kitchen. She remained in his view as she went to the sideboard and bent over to open its lower doors. She had her back towards him and her long straight legs, close together, reminded him of an advert he had seen for nylon stockings - only she wasn't wearing any. Her tiny mini skirt rode up, to display the briefest of frilly black panties Jim had ever seen. He was surprised to see so many freckles on the back of her thighs.

"I can't seem to find your books," she said without turning round. She appeared to be rummaging around on the bottom shelf of the sideboard. Jim knew that she always kept them in the top drawer, and he knew she knew that as well, but somehow he couldn't bring himself to remind her of it. It seemed obvious what she was doing, but now Jim began to have second thoughts about the situation he found himself in. Could it be a trap? Was her husband hiding behind the door waiting to pounce if he made advances towards her? The scandal would cause him to lose his

132

job. As he came up the path he had noticed that there were draped net curtains at the windows, but were they completely closed? Might someone be watching from another house? He was rooted to the spot not daring to move. He wanted to say something, but he hesitated too long searching for the right words. Eventually she straightened up and turned her head towards him. She remained looking at him for a while before speaking, and he was sure that she looked disappointed.

She said, quietly, "What shall we do now?" The button had come undone on her blouse and it was obvious to Jim that she wasn't wearing a bra.

Jim hesitated; he knew of a number of things he could say - wanted to say - but instead he answered lamely, "I could just take the money if you like, and then mark your books next time...."

"Mr Walker. MR WALKER." Jim turned his head, suddenly aware that it was Sheila calling to him. He drew a deep breath as he came out of his daydream. "Mrs Leyton has gone. She said goodbye to you twice but you obviously didn't hear her!"

Jim didn't answer. He thought it best to say nothing, but now she had gone he knew that it was the end of something that had not even begun.

NOT CRICKET?

Roy watched carefully, as Reynold's spin bowler took only three or four steps followed by a skip, before delivering his attempted off-break. It was short, turned only a fraction, and Roy met the ball in the middle of the bat lifting it over the square-leg boundary for a huge six.

Sitting on the grass outside the circle beyond deep-mid-on, young Alan clapped excitedly and then jumped up quickly to alter the scoreboard to 124. He turned to look at the captain of the batting side. "We only want four more to win, Dad."

Neither Roy, nor Tom at the other end of the wicket needed to move as they watched the ball clear the boundary chalk line to be caught by one of the few spectators standing on that side of the ground. It had been the last ball of the over, and, as the fielding side changed their positions, the two batsmen walked slowly towards each other.

"How are you gettin' on with your plans for the concert, Tom? Found a pianist yet?"

Tom shook his head. "No not yet, Roy. I'm still looking." He noticed that the captain had thrown the ball to their opening bowler. He chuckled.

"What does he think he's gonna to do," Roy said quietly out of the corner of his mouth. "We only need four to win! Just wait for the right ball, Tom, and we'll see this through."

Tom returned to his place at the crease and carefully took up his position as he watched their fastest bowler walk almost to the long off boundary before turning, then coming towards him like an express train. The first ball, which Tom left alone, was wide of the off stump, and then he heard the resounding slap when it arrived in the wicket-keeper's gloves. The second one was over-pitched, and he promptly dispatched it through extra cover to the boundary.

Amid a thin smattering of applause from the small crowd, Roy waited for his partner, and gave him a pat on the back as they walked off the field together towards the pavilion. "That wasn't a bad five wicket win, Tom. By the way, I think I might be able to help you with that pianist. I heard Rob Thompson talkin' about his sister the other day, and from what I could gather from his conversation, she could be the person you're lookin' for. She's somethin' of a musician, and quite a talented singer as well, I believe."

Tom turned quickly towards his friend. "I don't want a singer! I need a pianist!"

"Well alright, mate, but I gather that she plays the piano as well," Roy said quickly.

Tom's eyes opened wide as he again looked at Roy realising that his troubles could be nearly over. "The name rings a bell. Who's this Rob Thompson? or more importantly, when can I meet his sister?"

They had almost reached the wooden pavilion when they were greeted by their captain coming to give them a congratulatory handshake. "Good show fellas - both played well." He looked up at the overcast sky and at the dark clouds coming towards them from a westerly direction. "I think we did it in time - looks like rain coming."

As usual, the ladies had kept a watchful eye on the proceedings, and the tea was being made at the very moment they entered the hut. Dorothy Fielding thrust a plate of her tiny cheese and watercress sandwiches under Tom's nose even before he could put his bat down. He gave it to young Alan, the captain's son, who had followed them in and was looking at them in admiration. Tom took four of Mrs Fielding's sandwiches, and went over to where Roy was sitting, still in his pads and hungrily devouring one of Mrs. Dagworths lettuce and tomato 'doorsteps'. He took another bite and a large slice of wet tomato escaped from out of the side of his sandwich, and landed on to his still clean white flannels.

"Damn it." He looked up as Tom approached. "I thought they'd do for next week without being cleaned." He was smiling as he said it, treating his own clumsiness lightly. It crossed Tom's mind that Roy might not have done so if they had lost the match instead of winning it.

"I just remembered who that chap Rob is now," Tom said as he sat down. "He plays for the Winston Team. Do you think there's any chance of being able to call round tonight?"

"Call where?" Roy said, wiping the tomato off his trousers with his handkerchief, and spreading the red stain over an even bigger area than it had been to start with.

"To see that girl, whatever her name is."

"Oh, you mean Maureen." Roy took another bite out of his enormous sandwich, having eaten only half of it even after three mouthfuls. Tom had already completely devoured Mrs. Fielding's four.

"No good, old chap - not at this moment," he mumbled, his mouth full of lettuce and cucumber - the rest of the tomato had fallen out on to the other leg of his trousers -"I think I remember Rob tellin' me that she goes to Evensong at St. Mark's church every Sunday, so she won't be home until after half past seven. What time is it now?"

Tom looked at his watch. "Ten to six."

"Well, if its absolutely essential that you must go tonight, by the time we've eaten, had a wash and got changed, called in to the 'Dog and Partridge' for a quick jar, it'll be gettin' on for eight, and she should be home by then."

The next two hours seemed to drag for Tom, but he was the first to notice when it reached quarter-to-eight. "Isn't it time we got going?" he said quietly to Roy so that no one else would hear.

Roy looked up at the clock in the bar, and drained his glass. "Well, if we must, we must. Come on then. Let's get it over with. You won't be happy 'til you've asked her."

Maureen answered the door almost immediately after Roy had rang the bell.

"I'm sorry, Roy," she began, "but Rob's not here. I think he's..."

Roy didn't let her finish her sentence. "We don't want Rob, Maureen," he interrupted, "we've come to see you. This is Tom who would like a word with you. He wants to ask you a favour."

She looked at Tom and gave him a smile that lit up the whole of her face. Her eyes sparkled and she gave a little laugh as she spoke. "Sounds intriguing. You'd better come in."

Tom wasn't really listening as Roy explained to Maureen about the concert that he was going to do for the Darby and Joan Club, and his urgent need for someone to play the piano. Instead he was entranced; his attention captured by Maureen's beautiful blue alert eyes, highlighted by the expertly applied eye liner and eye shadow. Her perfect mouth was slightly open which kept breaking into little smiles as she listened to Roy's explanation, and when she did so, Tom was fascinated by the tiny creases which appeared along the sides of one of the prettiest noses he had ever seen.

As Roy finished, she clasped her hands together and turned to look at Tom. His heart stopped for a second or two. He couldn't believe that she was actually looking directly at him.

"I'm sorry, Tom, but I don't play that well. I couldn't possible do it I'm afraid."

If she had been a concert pianist, Tom would have accepted her refusal. She had said his name, and it didn't matter that she'd turned him down. He eventually found his voice to tell her that it was of no consequence and that he was certain to be able to find somebody else, and then added humbly, "I hope you didn't mind me asking you."

Maureen offered to make a coffee for them both, but Roy refused telling her that they must get back to their friends. As she rose from her chair, Tom took her hand into his and thanked her. He had an almost uncontrollable desire to give her a goodbye kiss as they left, but somehow managed to restrain himself.

"Whatever made you think that she could play that well?" Tom said sharply as they walked away from the house. He felt annoyed that Roy had put her in a position that might have been embarrassing, but at the same time was glad that he had met her. He was longing to see her again and already was trying to think of a plan for doing so.

Roy was saying something about noticing a piano in the house and knew that her brother didn't use it, and anyway, how was he to know that she couldn't play and what the hell was he worried about anyway, "You looked and acted as if you'd never seen a girl before! You can find your own pianist if that's all the thanks I get," he added, disgruntled at the way Tom had spoken to him.

Tom wasn't really listening to what his friend was saying as he couldn't get the girl out of his mind. "Well, you must admit that she's a bit stunning, and those blue eyes and her smile and......" Tom couldn't finish his sentence as he pictured her.

Roy read his thoughts. "I thought that you were lookin' for a pianist, not a conquest."

"I was just wondering whether she really meant what she said about not being able to play, or whether she was just being too modest," Tom said half to himself, and then added as if it was partly Roy's fault that he'd ruined everything, "I can't very well go back to the house to ask her again can I?"

Roy suddenly thought how he might be able to save the situation and help his friend who had either not believed the girl, or been pretty obviously infatuated with her. "Look, the Operatic Society is puttin' on a performance of 'The Mikado' in the Town Hall in a couple of weeks time, and she always takes part in their productions. If you really want to ask her again, why don't you go and talk to her after the performance. You can make it quite a casual meetin' if that's want you want," and then, as they got back into the car, he hoped that that was the end of the matter. "Now let's get back to the 'Dog' and have another pint with the boys. We've had a good win today. It's time to celebrate and forget all about women."

The next morning, Tom called into Lloyds Music Shop in the High Street, and booked a seat for the Friday night's performance of 'The Mikado'.

During the next two weeks he couldn't get her out of his mind, and it seemed an eternity before the day arrived when he had booked to see the show. Early on the Friday evening, he arrived at the Town Hall and bought a programme from a young teen-age girl in her school uniform. He turned to the page listing the cast and scanned through the principals. Perhaps Maureen will only be in the chorus, but then smiled broadly to himself when he saw her name against the role of 'Yum-Yum', one of the Three Little Maids'. He thought that that would be a good conversation starter, and hoped that she too would see the funny side of what he was now thinking. She certainly was 'yum-yum' in his eyes.

During the performance she sang and acted her part well and Tom thought that her voice was as beautiful as she was. Whenever she came on to the stage he saw no one else, and was certain that on at least two occasions she had looked straight at him. During the interval he boldly enquired whether it would be possible for him to talk to her, but was quite rightly refused permission unless it had been imperative for him to do so. He was also told that the producer of the show had expressly forbidden any of the cast to be seen off the stage in costume or make-up.

After the final curtain, he walked across the road with some of the audience to the "King's Head", and eventually managed to struggle through the mass of thirsty customers in the bar for a pint of ice-cold beer. It had been very hot in the theatre, and he was sweating, but probably more at the thought of soon being able to talk to the girl of his dreams, than because of the heat. After another twenty minutes or so had passed, he noticed that some of the cast had squeezed their way in and managed to get to the other end of the bar - remarkably quickly he thought. He noticed Maureen among them with a pint glass in her hand, drinking the contents faster than he could drink his, obviously wanting to quench her thirst after all that singing. They were all laughing and joking and having a good time; she seemingly being the centre of attention and the life and soul of the party. He decided that perhaps it wouldn't be quite the right time to approach her and finally went home feeling very disappointed of not having spoken to her. He had envied the fellows who had been with her, wishing that he had been one of them. It didn't really matter whether she could play the piano for him or not, he just had to see her again.

The following Sunday he made an excuse that he couldn't play in the cricket match and, in the evening, went to St. Mark's. The last time he had been to a church was to a funeral, and the time before that was when he was christened. He had remembered what Roy had told him about Maureen's regular attendance to evensong, and got there early to find a seat that would enable him to see her as soon as she entered the church. He bowed his head in prayer.

"Please God let her come: that she will see me: speak to me: perhaps sit next to me:"

He opened the deep maroon covered book on the shelf in front of him, and found "The Order for Evening Prayer," leaving it open at that page. He also opened the hymn book to the hymn number 745 as indicated on the board above the pulpit, and waited. He wondered where she usually sat, and whether she would come alone. He hadn't thought of that before. Perhaps she always came with another girl friend. He wouldn't allow himself to think that she might come with anyone else. He began to panic a little and felt his pulse racing. Perhaps he should have waited outside the church, or in the porch, to coincide with her arrival, and then they could have walked in together.

He was sure everyone looked at him as they came in and knew why he was there. He had telephoned Roy the day before, to tell him that he wouldn't be able to play today, but thought that Roy hadn't sounded fully convinced with his excuse. He was thankful that he hadn't pursued it as he had told his friend one lie, and didn't particularly want to tell him another.

More people arrived for the service and took their places. The organist was playing a piece of music which he thought he recognised, but as he was trying to remember what it was called, he was suddenly startled as the door was closed, the hollow clattering sound echoing throughout the church. The vicar appeared in the nave as the first notes of the processional hymn sounded. Tom stood up with the rest of the congregation but there was no Maureen. Where was she?

His disappointment engulfed him. Before the last verse began, he left his seat and crept silently out of the church.

"We missed you on Sunday, Tom." Roy had telephoned him at work, anxious to break the news of the team's defeat.

"We got slaughtered: lost by 95 runs! Where were you?"

"I told you on Saturday that I had to go up North to see my grandparents," Tom lied. The next lie he found easier to tell as it made the first one sound more plausible. "They're getting on a bit and wanted to see me."

"What are they gonna to do? Leave you all their money?"

Tom now felt less guilty when he realised that Roy had believed his story.

"By the way, Tom, did you see Maureen again on Friday? - and how did you like the show?"

The second question he answered easily but had to think a little longer how to answer the first. He didn't want to let Roy think that he'd only gone especially to see her. "Oh she was too involved with her friends to see me. It wasn't very important anyway." He knew that that was a bigger lie than the others he had told.

"Oh you'll soon find someone to play that damned piano," Roy assured him. "By the way, I saw Rob last night in the pub. He told me that his sister had been laid up all day with a sore throat. Too much singin' I expect." He laughed. "See you on Sunday, don't be late."

Tom put down the 'phone and smiled to himself, then quickly changed his expression when he realised that Maureen might not be feeling well. So that's why she hadn't turned up at church. He left his office early and called in at the florists on his way home. He asked the young girl to make up a large bouquet of pretty flowers, suitable for someone who was ill, and asked for them to be delivered immediately to the address he had written down. He had never sent flowers to anyone before, let alone a girl, and hoped that it was the right thing to do. Selecting a card from the rack in the shop, he wrote:

"To Yum-Yum. Hope you are feeling better. Still haven't found a pianist." He considered whether to put "Love", but thought better of it and signed it "Yours hopefully, Tom".

He meant the word 'hopefully' to mean that he hoped that she wanted to see him again as much as he wanted to see her, but he wondered whether she might just think that he still wanted her to play the piano.

Later that evening he began to have misgivings about whether he had done the right thing. His mind was in a turmoil. Sometimes he imagined her to be holding the flowers close to her, or looking at them lovingly as she lay in her sick bed. At other times he wondered whether she might be allergic to flowers, or that she might have known what he meant by that message and thrown them away. Perhaps he should have taken them to her himself and not chickened out by getting the florist to deliver them. Had he acted too spontaneously? Should he have waited until she knew him better?

It was a long time before he fell asleep and, when he did, Maureen was in his dreams. She was in his arms, her face pressed gently against his. He was telling her how much he loved her, but then she was running away from him and he was calling to her, and each time he got close she went further away, just out of his reach.

Tuesday morning began as quite a normal day for Tom, although Maureen was never out of his thoughts for a moment.

"There's a lady on the telephone asking to speak to you," Tom's secretary told him. "Shall I put her through?"

"Hello, is that you Tom?" said a quiet and slightly croaky voice.

"Who is that?" he asked, although the answer was superfluous as he knew at once that it was Maureen. He thought her voice sounded even more wonderful with the husky tones due to her sore throat.

"It's Maureen. I hope you don't mind me ringing you at work. I rang Roy first to see if he had your number. I just wanted to thank you for the flowers. It was a nice thought and they're my favourites. How did you know? I also wanted to tell you that I think I've found you a pianist."

Tom sat there listening to her as if in a trance. He was in love with her voice as much as he was in love with her, but when she stopped talking he was a little disappointed that she hadn't asked him what he had meant by putting 'hopefully' on the card.

"Hello, are you still there?" she enquired, getting no response from him.

"Yes, of course," Tom said hurriedly - was he really talking to her? - he wasn't thinking about pianists at this moment. "Can I call and see you?" he asked, boldly.

"Of course, then I can tell you about who I've got for you." Maureen had suddenly realised that she might have interrupted his busy routine. "I'm sorry, I shouldn't have telephoned you at work."

"No, no it's alright. Will you be in this evening about seven o'clock?"

Maureen said that she would, and Tom's last words were that he was glad she'd liked the flowers. He almost yelled out 'yippee' as he put down the phone, and for the rest of the day he was unable to concentrate fully on what he was doing. He tried to keep himself busy to prevent the day from seeming interminably long.

Tom sat outside Maureen's house at least ten minutes before the time he had arranged to call. The only other time he had felt as nervous as he did now was when he was waiting to bat, and the other side had a fast bowler who was taking all the wickets. He hoped he wasn't heading for defeat on this occasion. At precisely seven o'clock he rang her door bell.

Maureen answered the door almost immediately, and gave him a lovely smile as she invited him in. She was wearing a pretty flowery summer dress which did everything for her perfectly proportioned figure. He wanted to hold her in his arms, tell her how much he loved her and take her away into his dream world. He had made up his mind that he would tell her that he loved her and that they would spend the rest of their lives together.

"Now you sit there." Maureen pointed to an easy chair opposite to where she sat. He smiled to himself, as the way she had spoken to him was rather like being put into his fielding position by his captain.

"I've got someone who will be ideal for you what you want,"

she began. "He has played for me at many concerts and is a real musician....."

Tom was watching her as carefully as he did when a bowler came towards him down the wicket, but she was so pretty. He wasn't interested in her musician for the moment. He just wanted to reach out, hold her hands and tell her that he loved her.

"......and he's going to play the organ for me," she continued, "at my wedding in a month's time. I've written down his name, address and phone number for you."

She handed Tom a piece of paper but he just sat staring at her. The pit of his stomach felt hollow.

"Are you alright?" Maureen leaned forward to look at him more closely. "You've gone as white as a sheet."

Tom took the paper from her with a shaking hand. "Yes, I'm alright," he lied. "Her wedding in a month," she had said. He really felt completely defeated. She had sent down an impossible ball for him to play and bowled him first ball!

THE QUARRY

Leslie left school at Easter, two months after his fourteenth birthday. He had no idea how he was going to earn a living, and apart from being employed as an errand boy for a local grocery store, he had no knowledge of any other sort of work.

His elder brother, Daniel, was a clerk in the offices of a stone quarry situated in the high ground of the countryside a couple of miles out of town and, with his younger brother in mind, he considered that a junior clerk would be a great asset to the firm. It was 1942, and the quarry was supplying tarmac to the airfields which were being built at a rapid rate throughout the Midlands. This caused a lot more work in the office than previously, and Daniel thought that a junior clerk would relieve him of all the menial tasks that took up so much of his time. He put the suggestion to the Managing Director.

The M.D. was a man of huge stature. Always immaculately dressed in a three piece suit of good quality worsted cloth, a striped tie tied in a windsor knot, and a matching silk handkerchief in his top pocket, contrasting perfectly against his light blue Van Heusen shirt with its starched collar. His expensive leather shoes were always highly polished. When Leslie attended his interview for the job, the Managing Director invited him to sit beside him at his large mahogany desk and opened his ledgers. Leslie noticed how the figures had been impeccably written with a fountain pen in neat straight lines.

"You can add these columns easily, can't you?" he asked the young lad.

Leslie suddenly felt an emptiness in his stomach, and the blood drain from his face. Confronted with a page of pounds, shillings and pence, which he assumed he had been invited to total, he slowly began to add up aloud the pence column first.

"I don't want you to add up the figures," the Managing Director interjected, to Leslie's relief, "I'm pointing out to you how they should be written down to enable the columns to be added up easily and correctly, you see?"

Leslie also noted the beautiful copperplate writing. He hoped that he wasn't going to be expected to also write like that, or that his own untidy scrawl wouldn't be examined too closely if he was successful in getting the position of junior clerk.

All this had been almost two years ago, and Leslie was now part of the establishment. He was enjoying doing all the minor office tasks he was expected to do and for which he had been employed. Although paid very little for the work he did, he was happy in his job. His school days were long gone and forgotten, but in the new environment of a man's world, he was still very much a young boy with no experience of life. The thought had never crossed his mind that the quarrymen might not have enjoyed the work they were doing, or that their main incentive in coming to the quarry was the money they earned.

Whenever he could, he would leave the office, perhaps to do an errand for his brother, and visit the workshops or other buildings. It was in this way that he began to get acquainted with some of the workmen, and pretended not to be shocked when they used bad language, unaware that they did so deliberately for his benefit. He would take his time, perhaps to watch blacksmith Charlie Routledge, first make a shoe in the forge and then fit it, while it was still hot, on to one of the quarry horse's feet. Charlie, with a cigarette dangling from his lips, would blow through his large 'walrus' moustache - browned with nicotine stains - as he turned his head away from the smoke from the burning hoof, hammer in the nails and break off the points protruding through it with the fork end of his hammer. Then, using a large rasp, he would file the ends smooth to prevent them catching on anything. Leslie enjoyed the mixture of the pungent smells of burning hoof, steam, hot iron, and the coke fire, all of which contrasted sharply with the dusty dry smell of the granite clouds from the machinery, covering the whole area with a grey dust. He found all this invigorating and exciting.

Apart from the one locomotive which took the wagons to the lorry loading bay half-a-mile away, or the railway sidings further on, the horses were the only means of pulling the wagons to and from the quarry workings and around the machine plants.

Before returning to the office, Leslie would stop at the massive crusher plant where four men spent their working lives among the dust, and almost deafened by the incessant loud throbbing noise and vibrations of the heavy machinery. Approaching the narrow gauge railway line, he would sometimes wait to watch two of the heavy solid wooden wagons laden with rough blocks of blue granite, being pulled by a huge black stallion on to the crusher plant. After leaving the small weighbridge, squat little Jackie, his flat cap with the peak at the back, would run alongside, hitting the horse on the shank with his stick to ensure the animal pulled the heavy load to the top of the slope. Here, 'Tush' Taylor and Ted Larner, were waiting to drop the side of the wagons before tipping them over with a crow bar to allow the stone to fall out in a heap at their feet. Now they were able to feed the large lumps of granite with their bare hands into the hungry steel jaws of the double crusher. Leslie was amazed that lifting the heavy pieces of stone appeared to look so easy, and would dearly have loved to join them. He was convinced that it was the most important job in the quarry.

For the two men it was back-breaking work, but Leslie always found them ready to give him a cheerful smile as they carried out their heavy labours. As with most of the workers, they walked to the quarry early every morning and returned the same way after completing their eight hour working day. 'Tush' plodded his way by road on his large flat feet the one-and-a-half miles to his village, while Ted had a much more pleasant but longer journey through woods, across a meadow and a golf course, to the little grocery and confectionery shop where he lived with his family in the nearby town.

Underneath the crusher, amid the dust and noise, the other two men, Albert Bates and old Oliver Paxton, loaded the crushed stone into steel wagons from the hoppers above their heads. Leslie often stopped to watch Albert and Oliver who both worked in dreadful conditions. The thick grey dust covered their clothes, got into their mouths, throats and ears, and gave their faces a ghostly appearance. The noise made it impossible to speak or be heard, and was probably the cause of Oliver's deafness. He was a wonderful old man, full of character, and the lovely round vowels of his Gloucestershire accent, together with his pleasant nature, endeared him not only to Leslie, but to all of his workmates. His thick corduroy trousers were tied with string just below his knees to prevent the gritty dust from getting any further up his legs, and he wore a knotted piece of material around his neck. A battered cap protected his head, and, to the young clerk, the way he was dressed made him look every inch a real quarryman. Oliver and Albert hitched the wagons, now full of different size 'chippings', to the harness on a small brown mare, its colour now changed by the grey dust. The horse took some of the stone to Fred Hammond at the secondary crusher to be reduced further still. Leslie would then stroll to the tarmac plant which was worked by Ted Holtham and Bill Warwick, where the stone was covered with bitumen to produce 'bottoming' or 'topping' for the roads and airfields. The tar, after being heated to a high temperature to liquidize it, filled his young nostrils with its warm and addictive smell. The same boring things happened day after day, but to Leslie it was real adventure to walk around the plants watching all this activity taking place, unaware of the dangers and accidents that could happen.

On one particular day, the normal routine of everyday life at the quarry took on a different aspect. The events which occurred would change Leslie's outlook on life and take away the glamour of the work being done around him. It began quite normally. He had returned to the office after delivering a message which his brother had given to him to take to Frank Tillson in the stores. Frank was the quarry fitter and had requested a restocking of four-inch bolts for the wooden wagons. Back in the office, Leslie continued with the task of entering the weighbridge dockets from the previous day into their respective columns in the ledger. He was aware that the M.D. had come out of the other office and was standing with his back to the fire, his huge frame blocking out the heat from both him and his brother. The boss was tapping a Gold Flake cigarette on the back of his silver cigarette case to compress the loose tobacco, before putting it into his mouth and lighting it with the flame from his silver Ronson lighter which he had taken from his waistcoat pocket. Leslie was aware that they were about to hear another of his far-fetched stories.

"Had a couple of bloody cats sneaking round the pigeon loft for a couple of weeks after the chicks, but we caught the devils last night."

Leslie thought that he'd heard him tell a similar kind of story to this before, but he swivelled his chair round to face him, aware that the M.D. always liked an attentive audience when he related one of his stories.

"They were inside the damn loft - both of the bleeders." He drew deeply on his cigarette which he held tightly underneath the forefinger of his right hand - filled his lungs full of smoke and exhaled noisily. It always amused Leslie when he did this as it reminded him of a railway engine letting off steam.

"Watson was with me, so we grabbed hold of them, tied their bloody tails together and threw them over the clothes line."

Neither Leslie or his brother dared to show any sign of disbelief as they listened, and both remained expressionless.

"My god!" the M.D. continued, "You should have seen those cats fight - hissing and scratching each other - we daren't get anywhere near them." He chuckled as he related his story, his shoulders bouncing up and down, and occasionally drawing deeply on his cigarette. "'I picked up a sickle and sliced off their f...... tails." He moved his arm through the air in a horizontal arc as he re-enacted what he said that he had done. "They ran like hell across the paddock towards the cottages next to 'The Plough'." He chuckled again and then said thoughtfully, "I expect they belong to McKewan, the landlord. He'll think he's got a couple of Manx cats - but I bet they won't come back in a hurry!"

The two of them laughed with the M.D. more out of politeness than amusement. Leslie could never understand why he always swore, but nevertheless, pretended that he was quite used to hearing such language. They both knew that what he had told them was something that their boss would like to have carried out to the thieving felines that prowled round his pigeon loft, rather than what he had actually done. It was, however, understandable why he hated cats. The loft at the back of his house, 'The Paddock', had an excellent record for breeding young racing birds of good pedigree. He, and his loftsman, whom he always just referred to as Watson, were well-known and respected by other members of the local Flying Club, as regular winners of races, both in local and national competitions.

154

Leslie looked at the overweight, middle-aged Managing Director, slightly envying his lifestyle and the way he was always immaculately dressed. However, unlike himself who had a thick mop of brown hair kept under control with a liberal amount of Brylcreem, the M.D. was beginning to go grey and bald. What little hair he had was cut very short, but it gave him a neat and business-like appearance. However, Leslie thought that his manners often left a lot to be desired and, as if on cue, his boss dropped his chin to his chest, bent his knees, burped loudly, and simultaneously broke wind which reverberated around the room. As Leslie turned back to his desk to continue what he had been doing, a high pitched giggle came from the other office where his son, Kenneth, the Quarry Manager, was sitting at his desk sorting out the morning's mail. His father ignored him.

The Quarry Manager was the complete antithesis of his father: Oxford shirts, woollen check ties, sports jacket and corduroy trousers was his normal dress for work. He wore either strong brown leather boots or heavy shoes - usually not very well polished. Like his father, he too was almost bald, but what hair he had was very untidy. He was also smaller but more muscular, his rugged features and fresh complexion bearing evidence of the outdoor life he loved, always preferring to spend his time busying himself around the quarry than to sit in the office doing 'paperwork'. He was a man of action and had little time, or patience, for office administration, usually leaving the majority of the correspondence for his father to deal with. On occasions he would go out of the office with his double barrelled gun tucked under his arm, an old leather hold-all over his shoulder, and return an hour or so later with a bag full of rooks or a couple of rabbits.

A few days earlier the quarry had purchased a set of welding equipment for the first time, and very early that morning, Ken, (everyone always referred to him by his christian name) had tried it out in the blacksmith's shop by welding two thick pieces of steel together. Even before the metal had cooled properly, he had put one end in the vice and continued to hit the other end with a hammer trying to break it. He had been more than satisfied with the result.

"It began to crack below the weld!" he announced with a look of incredulity when he returned to the office.

Leslie was later aware that the quarry's other blacksmith, Ian McEwan, wasn't as enthusiastic about it as his employer was. Making an excuse to go to the stores, he had gone to have a look at what the Quarry Manager had done. Looking over his rimless spectacles at Leslie, the dour Scot had remarked that they had managed alright without this 'new fangled equipment' previously, "So what's so clever aboot it anyway?"

There was the sound of a shuffling of papers and the scraping of a chair across the wooden floor, and Ken emerged from the other office with his usual bustle. His father turned, threw the remainder of his cigarette into the fire, walked quickly back into his office and slammed the door.

Ken went through the correspondence with Daniel at an alarming rate, throwing the letters down on his desk with a quick "yes" or "no" in most cases, and a brief "tell them this," or "tell them that," in a few. He threw one over to Leslie with the words, "Here you are young 'un - have a go at this."

Leslie looked at the letter which was from the County Surveyor, H.L.Kent. It was a letter complaining about some tarmac which had been delivered, and Ken had written only one word across it - "Balls!". A buzzing sound interrupted his thoughts on how he should reply. He looked at the old fashioned telephone switchboard and at the celluloid number 5 which had dropped down. The call was from the quarry. Leslie picked up the ear piece from the hook on the candlestick telephone.

"Hello," came the familiar high pitched voice of the foreman.

He was only a small man, and Leslie could just picture him in his trilby hat, standing on tip toe in the wooden telephone box by the railway line at the entrance to the top pit. "Mr. Smith here. Is Ken there?"

The Quarry Manager had returned to his office, and Leslie put the call through to him and replaced the ear-piece on the hook. After a few minutes Ken came out of the office like an express train. He looked red in the face.

"It's those bloody I-ties (Italian prisoners of war) causing trouble again. First the hammers were too heavy, now the bloody shovels are too big for them! I've told Mr. Smith to get them all out immediately, and send them round by the blacksmith's shop and wait there." He turned to Leslie. "Get me the Commandant of the Camp at Maxstoke." He then spoke to Daniel. "They'll be coming out soon. Take them all back in the old Bedford, and tomorrow I'll go down to the German camp in Merevale Park and have a word with the Officer-in-Charge. Perhaps those Jerries will do better." Returning to his office, he too slammed the door.

"That door will come off its hinges one of these days," Daniel remarked as he left the office. Leslie dialled 'O' to get the girl on the exchange, then gave her the number he wanted and the quarry number. He always forgot to put the emphasis on the middle syllable of "Fillongley" as she always did, but he liked to hear her say it anyway. He imagined her as a pretty young thing, but it was possible that she might have been about 40 and married, so he had decided long ago that he would never risk flirting with any of the girls at the exchange. In any case, he wouldn't have dared to.

While waiting by the lorry, Daniel heard the sound of the foreman's bugle warning that explosive charges had been laid in the quarry face by the driller and shot-firer, and were soon to go off. The Italians were about to climb into the back to sit on the bench seats when the sounds of the explosion echoed down the valley. They began chattering excitedly to each other and Daniel couldn't decide whether they were glad to be leaving because of the war-like atmosphere of the quarry pit, or whether they were sorry. After all, during the months they had been at the quarry, they had been given a meat pie at midday to eat with the lunches that had been packed for them by the camp authorities, and, as they were not allowed to earn any money, Ken and his father had supplied them with cigarettes as an incentive to do the work. Perhaps some of them were suddenly realising that they would be losing these privileges due to the objections to the work by others, but it was too late: it had now been decided: they were all going back.

Daniel switched on the ignition, gave a couple of swings on the starting handle and the engine spluttered into life, shaking the body of the vehicle violently. With an occasional loud bang coming from the exhaust, the old lorry rattled its way at about twenty-five miles-per-hour down the rough tarmac road, arriving, eventually, at the P.O.W camp some ten miles away.

With all the excitement over, or so he thought, Leslie sat in front of the Remington Noiseless typewriter to compose his letter to the County Surveyor. He found it difficult to concentrate due to the raised voices coming from the other room. They were so loud that he couldn't help but overhear that the argument going on between the M.D. and his son, Ken, was about meat pies.

The loudest voice was that of the M.D. "And what the bloody hell do you think we're going to do with all those f...... pies now that you've sent the 'I-ties' back? Adcocks will have cooked them for us by now."

Leslie looked at the clock. It was noon. The door opened abruptly as the M.D. stormed out still putting on his hat and coat.

"We'll give them away to our men," shouted Ken, "The Italians would have got them for nothing anyway, so what's the difference?"

The M.D. grunted and went straight out of the office slamming the outside door so violently that the bay windows rattled. Ken gave another of his high-pitched giggles from his office. Usually, Leslie was invited to go with him to carry the trays containing the three dozen meat pies from Adcock's confectioner's and baker's shop. His boss had either forgotten to take him, or perhaps decided not to because it would have left no one in the office.

Half-an-hour later the M.D. returned in the same mood in which he had left. Striding across the office, he instructed the young clerk to get the trays from his car, and to sell the pies as usual for four pence each, but to give one away with each one sold. He closed his own door quietly as he entered his now empty office.

Leslie carried the hot pies to the large wooden hut where the men usually sat to eat their lunches. Inside there was a stove, unlit, three bare long wooden tables and five benches. The very tall figure of Tom Roberts from the top pit was already there together with George Kimber from the bottom pit. Tom collected the pies for himself and for the four others with whom he worked, and George bought a couple for himself and his mate. They were surprised, but delighted, to be carrying back twice as many as they had paid for.

The appetising smell of the hot meat pies made Leslie feel hungry as he watched the men from the workshops and machinery plant eating their 'snap'. The men cut up small lumps of cheese with their pen-knives, and, together with thick chunks of crusty bread and slices of Spam, ate their pies with relish, and drank cold tea from lemonade bottles. The hot pies that were left looked and smelt delicious.

Leslie opened his own pack of egg and tomato sandwiches which his mother had packed for him, put four pennies into the box next to the wooden tray, and took a mouthful of one of the meat pies. "Tush" Taylor from the crusher, gave him a toothless grin, then lost interest in what Leslie was doing as he continued to eat his own food with the few back teeth he had left. There were still five pies left unsold which Leslie took back to the office. The Managing Director was standing at the door in his hat and coat ready to leave as he watched him come up the path.

"How many do you have left, youngster?" He looked at the tray. "I'll take those with me for the dogs," he added, without waiting for a reply. Being a Monday, Leslie knew that he wouldn't return that day, as his racing pigeons would be returning during that afternoon to the loft at the back of his house. They had been released over the week-end, and, unless they had arrived back already, he and Watson would then be busy removing the rings from the first birds to return, putting them in the sealed clock, and taking it to the meeting point at the "Square and Compass".

After what had appeared to have been a hectic morning, the office was now quiet, so Leslie locked the door, put on a kettle of water to make himself a cup of tea, placed his completed letter to the County Surveyor on Ken's side of the desk in the other office, and helped himself to a Gold Flake cigarette from the large box on the M.D's side. After putting a few lumps of coal on the fire, he sat back in his brother's seat with his feet on the desk to enjoy the next hour on his own. He had no inkling of what lay in store for everyone that fateful afternoon.

Precisely at 1.30, the buzzer sounded on the switchboard and the number 6 disc dropped down. It was the lorry weighbridge down the road. Leslie flicked the lever and picked up the receiver and said "Hello."

"Arthur Faulkner here, is your brother there?" He'd recognised Leslie's voice and he sounded a little excited.

"No, not yet. He's gone to Fillongley," - Leslie put the emphasis on the middle syllable like the telephone operators did - "but he should be coming past you any minute, unless he's already done so. He's in the old Bedford."

"WD 168?"

"Yeah, that's the one. He took the prisoners back: surplus to requirements, Ken had said." Leslie had been longing to tell some of the men who wouldn't have known what had happened earlier, but Arthur appeared either not to have heard or had not understood his remark.

"Len Burrows has had another accident," Arthur was explaining, "but I think he's alright. Just sprained his ankle we think, and grazed his knees. Johnny Walters' lorry was here being weighed, so he put him in his cab and has taken him home."

"O.K. I'll tell Daniel when he gets back. How did it happen?"

"He'd just helped to load Johnny's lorry with some 'half-inch'. I'd finished the weighing, and then Len thought that he'd jump down on to the back of the lorry, but Johnny started to move on. He missed the lorry and landed on the weighbridge!"

Leslie was relieved that Len wasn't badly hurt, but unkindly almost burst out laughing as he imagined the scene. He thought that it was lucky that he hadn't broken a leg or even his neck.

"Oh!" Arthur interjected, "Daniel's just gone by while I'm talking to you, so I've missed him."

"Don't worry, I'll tell him what you've said when he comes in."

"Well that's the last journey I'll be making to Fillongley, or Maxstoke rather," Daniel announced as he entered the office.

His brother wasn't listening. "You'll never guess what Len Burrows has done," Leslie said excitedly. He could hardly restrain himself from bursting out laughing.

"Not another accident?" Daniel enquired. It had only been a few weeks since Len had been standing in a hopper raking the chippings when someone had opened the door below not knowing he was there. He went down with the stone and had been buried up to his neck in the back of the lorry. He had to be dug out, much to the amusement of everyone except Len. Fortunately, he escaped with only cuts and bruises.

"What happened this time?"

Leslie repeated what Arthur had told him.

"He'll get himself killed before long," Daniel said, under his breath. He went to the telephone, spoke to Arthur Faulkner, and got the full story first hand. He then put the report into the accident book, unaware that he would have two more to enter before the day was through.

The next half an hour passed quietly with Leslie finishing off the weighbridge slips and Daniel starting on the long process of calculating the men's weekly wages for those on piece-work, for the others it was easier. According to the foreman's time-sheets, most men on the 'flat daily rate' had put in a full week's work: forty-eight and three quarter hours at two shillings an hour totalling four pounds, seventeen shillings and sixpence. It was a simple sum to work out. The weather had been fine last week so there was no 'wet time' to add. If it had rained, 'wet time' would have reduced this figure considerably, since the rate was only eightpence an hour when heavy rain made it impossible for the men to work outside.

Leslie got up from his chair to stretch his legs. He considered that sitting down for half an hour at a time was long enough, especially when neither of the bosses were about. He looked out of the bay window towards the crushers and watched Jackie beating the big black stallion, somewhat unmercifully he thought, with the short stick that he always carried, in an attempt to get the poor creature to pull the heavy wagons much quicker from the small weighbridge and on to the crusher platform.

"He's hitting him again, Daniel. And now he's grabbed the bridle and he's running in front trying to pull the horse along...Oh! my god!" Leslie's sudden exclamation caused his brother to leap from his chair to join him at the window.

The horse had stopped and had grabbed his cruel mentor by the nose, shaking his head from side to side. They could hear Jackie screaming and shouting as soon as the horse let go of him.

"He's been asking for that," Daniel muttered as he went towards the door.

"He's running this way." Leslie shouted, "and his face is covered in blood!"

The horse had pushed Jackie away and was pawing the ground with its front hoof, shaking its head in up and down movements, snorting and showing all its teeth. Daniel changed his decision to go down, and instead, took the large first-aid box off the shelf as Jackie came bursting into the office. His hand covered his face and blood was squeezing out between his fingers and running down his arm.

"The bloody 'orse 'as bitten me nose off," he screamed in despair and fell back on to the nearest chair. Leslie daren't look and felt sick, but Daniel sent him to fetch a bowl of water as he grabbed a wad of lint from the box.

"Let's have a look." Daniel slowly lifted Jackie's hand from his face. "No, you're alright. The nose is still there, but it will probably be twice as big tomorrow. It's cut rather badly."

The Quarry Manager came into the office just before Daniel had completed the cleaning up of Jackie's face. He was out of breath and obviously had run a long way. He looked at Jackie, and saw a large wad of lint covering his nose, held down by strips of elastoplast. Daniel had plugged his nostrils with cotton wool and traces of dried blood were still on his face, hands and clothing.

"There's a story going round the quarry that the horse bit your face off!" Ken tactlessly remarked. Jackie went pale at the thought of what might have happened, and Leslie suddenly felt sick again.

"He needs to go for treatment," Daniel told his boss quietly, "I think he needs a few stitches in that nose."

Ken looked at the pathetic figure in the chair. He was one of his long-serving employees and had been at the quarry ever since he left school at the age of fourteen.

"Come on then, my lad, we'll take a trip to the doctor."

Daniel reached for the accident book as they left.

"I'd better go and re-organise the workforce down below," he said thoughtfully.

Leslie was looking out the window to see what was happening at the weighbridge.

"No need to," he remarked, "Herbie's doing it." Herbie Ireland was the odd job man at the quarry, and he also knew how to handle the horses and was ready to do Jackie's job. Meanwhile Herbie was explaining what had happened to George Brown, who brought the loaded wagons from the pits to the weighbridge. George was patting his own horse's neck as he listened to the story. His was a very placid mare and had a much easier life bringing the full wagons on the rail track down the gentle slope from the quarry. Although it was uphill on the way back to the pits, the wagons were empty, and overall it was much lighter work than Jackie's stallion had to perform.

"Right then, Leslie, we'd better get back to work and do the letters before Ken gets back."

"I've done mine, and I've put it on Ken's desk. The copy's in front of you. Is it alright?" now feeling a little unsure of what he'd written. Daniel quickly read both the letter and the reply.

"Hm! it'll do, but you'd better do it again and this time put, 'Yours truly' not 'sincerely'." He then added, "Don't forget, 'sincerely' after 'Dear Mr. so and so,' and 'truly'-or 'faithfully'- after 'Dear Sir.' O.K.?"

Leslie swore under his breath. He'd have to type the whole thing again.

"And when you've done that," his brother added, "you can go and find out when Bill Hammond wants another supply of oats for the horses."

Leslie loved going to the stables, but was pleased that he didn't have to go straight away, as he found himself shaking a little after the recent events. He tried to concentrate on re-writing his letter.

164

'Daer Sir,' he began. "Damn," he said out loud. He put a fresh letterhead in the machine.

'Dear Sor,' "I've done it again," he shouted. He got it right the third time and re-typed the letter very carefully. He then replaced the one on the Quarry Manager's desk with the new one, gave the copy to his brother, and, now feeling himself again, was out of the office before Daniel had chance to pick up the letter to check if he had done it correctly. Leslie hoped that Bill would be standing at one of the stable doors with just the head and neck of a horse looking out over his shoulder, as if posing for a photograph. He always imagined the stable scene to be like that: almost an exact replica of a picture in a book he had at home of Captain Oates leaning on a stable door with the horses in his care, during Scott's South Pole adventure. Leslie ran quickly to the stables to enable him to spend more time with Bill.

Bernard Masters, standing on the footplate of his loco, watched as Leslie crossed the railway line between the steel Granby wagons loaded with different sizes of stone. His 60 ton, 0-6-0 Hunslet locomotive, had built up sufficient steam to enable it to pull the heavy wagons half a mile down the road to the place where the lorries were loaded and weighed, and then to return with a long line of empties. Bernard was wiping his hands on an oily rag, the smoke from his pipe competing with the smoke from the chimney on his machine. He deliberately gave a short loud blast on the whistle and Leslie nearly jumped out of his skin. He'd never even noticed the engine or Bernard: his mind had been on where he was going and all that had happened that afternoon.

Arriving at the stables he found Bill sweeping out the bays with a huge yard brush. The smell of horses, fresh straw and horse dung mingled together and filled his nostrils. It was a smell that he never found unpleasant. Indeed, he loved it, and if Bill had given him the brush and told him to 'carry on,' he would have welcomed the task.

"Did you hear about Jackie?" Leslie thought that at least Bill would have some sympathy with the stallion rather than with his work-mate.

Bill nodded without committing himself one way or the other. "I saw him going off with Ken in the car; has he taken him home?"

"He's gone to the doctor's - needs a few stitches in his nose and it serves him right." Surely Bill would agree with that sentiment: he must have seen weals occasionally on the horse's flanks at the end of the day.

Bill carried on sweeping and glanced up at his visitor. "I don't believe he's ever really hurt that horse."

Leslie was surprised at that statement, especially coming from Bill. "Well, why does he do it then?"

Bill stopped what he was doing, put his hands together on the top of the brush handle, rested his chin on his hands and looked at the young innocent lad. Leslie knew that Bill knew everything you wanted to know about horses.

"That horse knows his job," Bill began. "He knows what he has to do and does it all day long. He doesn't need to be told - and certainly not forced. But he'd just had enough of the stick and it was his way of telling Jackie. The horse didn't know what he'd done! If he'd really wanted to hurt him, he'd have kicked Jackie from here to kingdom come - and he'd have finished up with more than a bloody nose!"

Bill turned away and carried on with what he was doing. "So what did you want me for?" he added.

"Daniel wants to know when you want some more oats delivered." After Bill had given him his answer, Leslie walked away from the stables deep in thought. He stopped to look back and saw Bill leaning on the stable door. Leslie gave him a wave and Bill lifted up his brush. He wished he knew as much about horses as Bill did.

Bernard had taken the train on its last journey of the day, and puffs of white smoke rose above the trees as it made its way down the track. It occurred to Leslie that it was unusual to still hear the sound of the engine all that distance away, then he was aware of how quiet it was. There was not the usual noisy rhythmic drumming of the machinery at the crusher plant. The white dust had stopped belching out of the chimneys. It was too early in the afternoon for the engines to be switched off, but they were quiet now.

"What's happened?" Bill shouted. His voice seemed unusually loud in the silence.

Leslie shrugged his shoulders. "Don't know." There was a crowd of men underneath the crushers and he noticed that the two men from the secondary crusher were running in that direction. Terrible thoughts went through Leslie's mind as he sprinted after them. There must have been an accident, and a serious one at that, for the machinery to be stopped. Then he was at the scene and he didn't like what he saw. Poor old Oliver lay on the ground between two steel wagons. Both legs were obviously very badly damaged just below the knees and his feet were turned inwards. His corduroy trousers, thick with white dust were torn and covered with blood. Two of his workmates were trying to lift him off the track. His right foot didn't move. Oliver cried out. His hands looked lifeless, his mouth was open and his eyes closed. He was obviously in a lot of pain and barely conscious.

"Don't move him," Daniel said as he arrived after running down the slope from the office. "I've 'phoned for the ambulance. We must try and make him comfortable. Just keep him warm and I'll try to stop the bleeding."

Someone put a jacket under Oliver's head and another put one across his body. Daniel quickly made a make-shift tourniquet, and placed it against the pressure point on the inside of the thigh of Oliver's right leg which was bleeding profusely. The other leg looked the wrong way round and there was some blood coming from that one too. Daniel looked at his watch and made a mental note of the time. He'd read that somewhere about applying tourniquets. Leslie suddenly felt terribly sick for the second time that day, and made his way slowly back to the office, his eyes full of tears. He couldn't bear to see poor old Oliver in pain. He was such a grand old man and a dedicated workman. He knew that he'd walked the two miles to work that morning as usual, across the countryside which he loved, but now his walking days were over, and possibly his life. Leslie couldn't bear to think about it any more. The quarry suddenly took on a different aspect and there was a sinister feeling about the place.

Fifteen minutes later, he heard the ambulance arrive - it seemed a lot longer than that to Leslie. Daniel came back to the office looking tired and flopped back into his chair. The clock on the mantelpiece struck four.

"They've taken him off," Daniel said quietly, "but he's not too good. He'll certainly lose his right leg and the other one looked pretty bad."

"What happened? "Do you know?"

"It looks as if the horse pulled the two empties up the slope as usual, and then Oliver changed the points and went back underneath to fill the wagon under the hopper. The chain behind the horse must have gone slack, came unhooked from the empties and they rolled back down the slope at speed, trapping Oliver between the empty ones and the full one underneath. He wouldn't hear anything because of the noise, and especially being so deaf." Daniel paused in his explanation, as if trying to imagine the sequence of events and how it could be prevented from happening in the future. He knew that Oliver and Albert were both so careful usually.

"Albert said that at the last seconds he had seen what was about to happen and shouted, but he was too far away to do anything.

Oliver obviously didn't hear him."

Neither spoke for a couple of minutes. There was nothing left to say, and Leslie went outside to get some air. The Quarry Manager had been at the scene when the Ambulance had arrived, and was walking slowly up the path towards the office. He said nothing as he passed by, and Leslie followed him in.

Ken glanced at Daniel. "I've sent them all home," he said, then went into his office and closed the door quietly. Leslie heard the click on the switchboard indicating that Ken had picked up the telephone. He was no doubt telephoning his father about the tragedy.

Daniel was writing again in the accident book, and Leslie noticed that he had tears in his eyes.

"Strange how these things always seem to happen in threes," he remarked.

Three weeks later, Oliver died. Both of his legs had been amputated immediately below the knee, and he never fully recovered from the operations. It had all been too much for him to endure at his age. Leslie accepted an invitation from his two daughters whom he had lived with, to go and see him.

He had never seen a dead person before but knew that he would always remember Oliver as he had always known him: in his work clothes, covered in grey quarry dust, plodding along with the horse or turning the metal wheels of the hoppers and filling the steel wagons with stone chippings.

Leslie was surprised how peaceful he looked lying there in the satin lined coffin, his long white hair beautifully groomed and his moustache immaculate and symmetrical, all devoid of any traces of grey quarry dust, the whiteness contrasting against his rouge tinted cheeks. His face was an exact wax like copy of the real Oliver and he bore the trace of a smile, looking a lot younger than his seventy years. Leslie's eyes filled with tears until he could no longer see the old man clearly.

Oliver's funeral was attended by most of his workmates dressed in suits and, to Leslie, not looking at all like quarrymen. At the quarry next day, everyone carried on working as if nothing had happened, but he missed the old man, and Leslie didn't have that same thrill at watching the other men at work on the crusher plant as he had before. He suddenly felt a lot older than his sixteen years. He had grown up that day, and left his boyhood for ever.

TEA FOR TWO...

It was early April, 1972. David and Tracy were staying at a guest house in Lynton. The small holiday town situated some 500 feet above the small picturesque village of Lynmouth on the North Devon coast had been chosen by the couple as the place to spend their honeymoon. From the summit of Summerhouse Hill the scenery was breathtaking, and below, at the mouth of the East Lyn, Lynmouth's tiny harbour was filled with small boats waiting to put out to sea at the turn of the tide. The rocky coastline and surrounding countryside had a beauty of its own, and there was much to explore. The pale yellow of the early primroses, abundant beneath the trees in the woodlands and on the high banks along sunken roads, heralded the sweet freshness of Spring. There was a poetic charm about the surrounding small villages serenely resting and ageing gracefully in the folds of the hills. Scattered houses perched on the hillside overlooking the sea, glistening white in the sunlight amidst the shades of green of the trees perpendicular on the steep slopes.

In nearby Somerset, the young couple visited Selworthy with its white-painted cottages - grouped in an attractive but disorderly fashion around a butterfly-shaped green. Their red-brick chimneys, built tall to protect the thatched roofs from catching alight from sparks at the time when open fires burned in their grates, stood like sentries guarding this beautifully preserved village.

Leaving the village, they stopped to admire the double-arched Packhorse Bridge at Allerford, then continued into the lovely village of Bossington. Here they stood in front of a pretty little tea-shop which had previously been the village bakehouse with its low doorway, requiring them to bow their heads in order to enter and, once inside, they discovered an Aladdin's Cave. Fine English china and beautifully decorated ornaments filled the shelves, while families of tiny mice, intricately made from sheep's wool, peered about them with their beady black eyes wide open, as they sat on display in small groups eagerly waiting to be purchased by the visitors. The couple drank their tea from delicate Coalport china cups, and ate home made cakes and scones, deliciously light, served with yellow butter, clotted cream and strawberry jam. They sat for a long time in those unique and magical surroundings, discovering even more treasures around them as their eyes scanned every corner of the room. There were exquisitely hand painted china ornaments and birds, water colours of the surrounding countryside and coastal scenes by local artists, and many other tempting gifts to admire as they relaxed in the peaceful atmosphere and tranquillity of the delightful tea-shop.

Next day they travelled by car along the Lynmouth to Porlock road, and turned on to the Worthy toll-road opposite the ancient and historical Culbone Stables Inn. Small plantations of old stunted pine trees, their trunks gnarled with age, stood like carved statues behind a post-and-wire fence bordering the road, and, further on in the meadows, the hardy North Devon sheep grazed lazily in the early morning sunshine. As they descended the hill, the narrow road twisted and wormed its way through dark woodland alongside a small stream which rippled over its rough stony bed. A grassy bank scattered with tree boles and the occasional boulder, guarded the water's edge from damage by the wheels of passing vehicles.

After parking their car close to the toll-gate house, they climbed and walked along a path for a mile and a half through Yarner woods towards Culbone. Through the tall mottled white trunks of silver birch, interspersed with beech, hazel, conifer, and fallen trees rotting in the deep undergrowth, they looked down to the sea shrouded in a ghostly mist hundreds of feet below. The air was still, and hardly a sound could be heard except for their own footsteps, the sweet-sharp prolonged notes of the song of the robin, and the shrill call of an occasional blackbird sounding its machine-gun-like burst as it flew away disturbed by their presence. A stoat suddenly appeared on the path ahead; they stood perfectly still; it lifted its head sniffing, caught their scent, then scurried away into the undergrowth. Now, descending along the worn path towards their destination, they could see glimpses of the tiny Culbone church through the trees on the opposite side of the narrow valley, and listened to the tinkling sounds of a fast-moving stream as it tumbled over the rocks to the sea still some 500 feet below. The early sun had not yet reached this remote place, which was sheltered from the winds often blowing fiercely across the moors high over the hill. In the still air, the only sounds were the babbling waters and the melody of bird song echoing through the trees.

Crossing the old narrow bridge, and passing by the few cottages nestling at the side of the stream, they found that they were the sole visitors to the church that morning, in this smallest complete parish of the British Isles. Opening the door quietly, they sat for a while on the old unpolished wooden pews, admiring the 14th century screen, and noting the dates and times when the services were being held for this remote and tiny community.

The path behind the church led to a small isolated cottage, and from its tall chimney, smoke spiralled, filtering through the trees as if searching to find the clear open sky above. On the other side of a little wooden gate they noticed a sign saying 'Teas', and making their way to the tea-garden past the door of the house, they were greeted by a little old lady who introduced herself as Lizzie Cook. The unstained wooden garden-furniture looked well weathered, and on each of the tables was a jam-jar of wild flowers. They sat in the midst of her pretty cottage-garden; the blues of the aubretias and the many rich colours of the polyanthus in full bloom. On a bird table nearby, blue tits and great tits pecked industriously at strings of peanuts, whilst a small party of house sparrows and a pair of chaffinches hopped around on the ground, their heads bobbing and jerking, pecking at anything they could find. Not wishing to disturb the peace, the couple sat in silence as they waited for their tea to arrive, allowing themselves a few moments to reflect on the tranquillity of this delightful scene.

The old lady walked carefully towards them wearing a clean flowery apron, carrying their tea on a tray containing an assortment of unmatched crockery.

"There you are, m'dears," she said in her lovely rich North Somerset tones, as she placed a plate of a few home made biscuits on the table. "You won't forget to sign my visitors' book before you go will you?"

They were still the only customers so far that morning, and they wondered how many other visitors the old lady served with tea throughout the year. "Do you get many people here?" Tracy asked.

"Oh I get quite a few during the season," she replied, as she laid the pots carefully on the table, then added proudly, "and from all over the world! I can just about manage to cater for a coach load when they arrive after they've walked through the wood. I've got plenty of cups and teapots." She smiled and turned to go back to the cottage carrying the now empty tray. "Enjoy your tea, m'dears."

They looked around in disbelief. 'A coach load' she had said!

Where would they all sit? the girl wondered, whispering her remarks so as not to let the old lady hear for fear of hurting her feelings.

It was so calm and peaceful as they sat enjoying their tea, and felt no particular desire to hurry. Indeed, time appeared to have no significance in the quiet serenity of the garden. A green woodpecker flew across the narrow valley in its undulating flight, its conspicuous yellow-green rump and red crown, catching the thin long-fingered rays of sunlight now beginning to filter through the trees.

They signed her visitors' book as they left, adding to the list of unfamiliar names of people from places as far away as Japan, the USA, as well as Europe and the British Isles. As they wrote their names, she told them of the many greeting cards she received at Christmas from all over the world.

Her little cottage had possibly not altered for many decades. Its 300-year-old walls and stone sill windows added to its attraction, and, inside, they noticed that on the range fireplace, a kettle of hot water sat waiting for the next customers to arrive. There were many cups, saucers, plates and teapots, well positioned to be easily accessible, and a couple of plates on the table containing home made cakes which she had probably made that morning.

"How much do we owe you?" David asked in the absence of a bill.

"Oh, sixpence," she said, shrugging her shoulders as if it almost embarrassed to even ask for that.

"Sixpence!" David repeated with surprised amusement. "Don't you realise that we're now decimalised," he added kindly.

"Oh, I can't be bothered with that," she said dismissively. "I don't understand that new money."

The young man put two 10p coins into her hand which to him seemed fair, and then, as they walked away, he suddenly realised that he'd given her eight times what she'd asked for!

They turned to give her a little wave as she stood at her door watching them go down the path away from the house. She was smiling and gave a little wave back.

"I bet she says that to all her customers," he said.

...or THREE

The following day, David planned a circular walk from the small car park near the Woody Bay Hotel, along the coastal path to Hunter's Inn, then back along the road to where they would leave their car.

It was a lovely day and, wishing to carry as little as possible they set off with anoraks tied around their waists should the weather change, and a small rucksack containing some food and essentials for the journey, knowing that they would be able to get something to eat when they reached Hunter's Inn some six or seven miles away. They set off along the higher of the two coastal paths soon to negotiate the tricky deep cleft on the rocky cliff face at 'Hollow Brook', but being rewarded with uninterrupted views across the Bristol Channel to the South Wales coast line in the distance. They found the cliff walk exciting and invigorating, and were thankful that they were wearing their strong climbing boots on the sometimes difficult stony path. Eventually they reached Heddons Mouth Cleave, and walked along the valley through the trees to Hunter's Inn.

Over a pint of rough cider and a plate of sandwiches, and after a long rest from their exertions, they took the very steep road towards the village of Martinhoe. Two or three cars passed them with their high pitched engines whirling away in first gear on the 1-in-4 hill - it seemed even steeper than that on foot - and eventually they reached the village of Martinhoe. Some years earlier, David had remembered a small tea-room there, but when he found the house it was no longer the place it had been. What appeared to be the old sign, lay on the grass behind a rickety wooden gate. In the untidy garden stooped a figure, fork in hand, digging out some grass and weeds from among some unpruned roses. David was surprised to see wellingtons being worn, and an old trilby hat and long coat, in view of the dry ground and heat of the day.

He called out to enquire whether this was the place that used to be "The Galleon," and whether tea was still available and the bent figure stood up and faced him. They were surprised to hear a woman's voice telling them that it was no longer a tea-room and, since the day when she had bought the place, they were the first to enquire whether it still was. However, she took pity on the two apparently exhausted looking travellers, and said that she would make them a cup of tea if they would like to come in to the house, as she herself could do with one.

The hall entrance was littered with cardboard boxes, and models of ships and galleons lay on the shelves covered in dust. She invited them to sit down in the living room, and finding an old but comfortable settee, they rested their weary bones as the lady left to make the tea. They noticed more unpacked boxes and concluded that she obviously hadn't been long in the house. In the hearth was a huge fire-screen in the shape of an old penny shielding the empty grate. She returned quite quickly with a large pot of tea on a tray, with milk, sugar, and three cups and saucers and, placing the tray in front of Tracy, sat down heavily and wearily in a large easy chair opposite them.

"Would you like to pour one for me when you pour yours, m'dear?" she asked, and then, throwing off her trilby hat, she revealed herself to be a woman in her fifties, and with a very healthy complexion. I'm sorry about the mess," she said apologetically, "but I haven't had time to unpack everything since I moved here from Berryharbour."

David smiled knowingly, in confirmation of his first impressions that she'd recently moved. "You haven't been here long then?" he asked confidently.

Her reply took them so much by surprise that they almost spluttered into the cups they were drinking from.

"Oh no," she said, "...only ten years!"

They laughed all the way back to the car.